1. Fortune favours the brave

"So, you read my article," asked Andrew. "What did you think?"

"You're an idiot, brother," replied Eustace, "you always have been."

They were sat on a bench in the square next to Eustace's hotel. Andrew had managed to corner Eustace as the slightly older man was making his way over to the adjacent car park.

"You're the one's been sniffing around father's friends at the conservative club. Is that why you came all this way: to advise the blue rinse brigade on their stock options? Or do they really believe they're going to get their local candidate in? Perhaps you know something we don't, now you're in the civil service."

"I honestly believe you write those articles just to annoy father. Or so that your friends at the council think you're the right sort of fellow. Mother still adores you though, she knows what side you'll be on when the chips are down."

"Was Vollet at the club? Still trying to push his propaganda through the Gazette. A forlorn hope in this territory, why does he do it?"

"Vollet isn't as stupid as he looks."

"You DO know something. Tell me."

Eustace merely smiled tolerantly and patted his brother on the knee. "I'll be in touch," he said, then picked up his luggage and got up from the bench. Andrew watched him cross the precinct, then scowled at some pigeons who were pecking at crumbs nearby. There was something unorthodox about his brother's spree of recent visits, but for some reason he was being kept out of the loop. He sensed that it meant money, of which he was rather short: his wife complaining that they needed a bigger house. Well, he would just have to keep his eyes open and make sure he had a seat at the table, when the time came.

Before heading back to the city, Eustace called on his parents one last time. They lived in a semi detached house. It was respectable enough, but far more modest than you might expect for the owners of a local engineering firm. The business though, since the late 1970s, had become mired in one struggle after another, and most of the money it did make his mother Fiona had decided to re-invest in the children's education, sending Andrew and Eustace to Bristol, Philip and Simone to Kings: a venture that so far had failed to live up to their expectations - all their children having mid level careers or mid level spouses. Eventually they had resigned themselves also to the failure of the business - Puesch and Barlow: it had been started up by Fiona's family at the beginning of the 1800s. The first episode of bankruptcy had come around in the 1960s and that was how her husband Peter had bought his way in, investing a hefty bunch of cash to save it from closure. Her grateful father and uncle had handed the pair of them the reins, and at first, they had been able to modernise the factory, reviving somewhat its fortunes. In the end though, cheap rival imports and labour

The Aviary
Part one

Wendell Harris

Copyright © 2024 Wendell Harris All rights reserved

The characters and events portrayed in this book are fictitious. Any similarity to real persons, living or dead, is coincidental and not intended by the author.

No part of this book may be reproduced, or stored in a retrieval system, or transmitted in any form or by any means, electronic, mechanical, photocopying, recording, or otherwise, without express written permission of the publisher.

"They said it was the beginning of a permissive new age

But now it's just the same old cabbage"

Mark Smith, Mess of my Age

disputes had made it impossible to stay afloat and they had ended up cashing in the business so as to afford a reasonably comfortable early retirement. Still, they were rueful, and had come to hope that by playing politics, trading on their lingering influence among the working folk of the town, they might belatedly achieve the level of success and respectability they felt they really deserved. So far, this had meant trying to drum up support for the conservatives in a die hard labour town.

Now Fiona was sat in their tastefully appointed living room with its floral wallpaper and soft Laura Ashley furnishings, while Peter and Eustace covertly discussed last minute 'strategy' upstairs. Such secrecy was annoying, as though she hadn't been the one who'd made half the decisions concerning the factory when it was operational. Eventually she heard them murmur louder as a door opened and they came out of the bedroom onto the upstairs landing. She went out into the hallway in order to make her farewells.

"You understand," Eustace was saying as they reached the head of the staircase, "that's the way the wind is blowing and people who give their support early will be rewarded."

"And what have you two been plotting?" she asked.

"All in good time mother," declared Eustace. "Just a few more choice tidbits I wanted to share with father."

His attempts to vex her were deliberate of course, but then she had always favoured Andrew who in her opinion showed flair, while Eustace to her had seemed like more of a plodder. He came down the stairs, put his hand on her arm and kissed her cheek and then picked up his luggage and opened the front door, but just as he was halfway through turned around and said, "And whatever you do father, don't discuss this with Andrew. He'll make a mess of it. Best to let him scrounge his own portion once it's all settled." And then he left.

She turned to look at Peter, who was still only halfway down the staircase. "So, what WAS that all about?" she asked.

"I promised not to say too much," he replied, "although .. how do you fancy being married to a member of the Endorsement Committee."

She looked at him with puzzled amusement. "Endorsement Committee, what's that?" she asked.

"It would be a non government role, sort of a link between the local councils and Whitehall. The funny thing is, it would carry more actual clout than an elected position, according to Eustace."

"Really, and what would you have to do?"

"Back the right horse, that's all. There are whispers in the corridors of power that the Tories have had their day and that the socialists are running on a more progressive platform. There's this new man: Blunt. He's sleek, appeals to the professional classes."

The Conservative club was an anonymous red brick building adjacent to a park, resembling nothing better than a pool hall or a working men's club. In its modesty it hoped to appeal to the low key aspirations of the populace. The interior was appointed in a similar manner, with its bar selling discounted ales, dartboard, its orange worn and scratched vinyl seats and its sporting posters. In the upstairs 'debating' room, the atmosphere was more exclusive, snug and smoky, with its leather bound armchairs, thick carpet and good whisky.

"Does your son enjoy printing this kind of thing," asked Roberts, the estate agent. He was referring to an article in The Worker by Andrew which accused the local Gazette of being 'a mouthpiece of the speculators'.

"The worst thing is," added Councillor Sykes, "you talked me into letting him marry my daughter. I thought you said he'd grow out of that student reactionary nonsense."

"He will," said Peter, "it's just taking longer than expected."

"Ten bloody years."

"Your other son though," said Roberts. "He seems to have his head screwed on. What's this he says about the socialists modernising their party?"

"They've been trying to do that for a decade," put in Garland, the carpet wholesaler. "No one's fooled. The unions have an iron grip."

"I wouldn't be too sure," said Peter. "I've got more reason to be skeptical than anyone, after what the unions did to my factory, but there's this new man, Bland. A lot of the younger members are putting their weight behind him. These are the ones who grew up students instead of workers, their values are inherently more bourgeois."

"Interesting," said Vollet.

"One or two articles, saying that this chap is a step in the right direction for the socialists. We don't throw our weight behind him, you understand. Just enough so that if he's made head of the party we'll be remembered."

"Do we want to be remembered that way though?" said Roberts "And what are his chances anyway?"

Although everyone in the room was smartly attired, only one of the people present could be said to be tailored, and that was the elderly stockbroker Cranshaw. He had been a friend of Fiona's parents and two years back had joined the club at Peter's request. "You're the ones with the ear of the locals Peter," he said, stubbing out a cigarette in a heavy black ashtray. "What do you reckon?"

"I think they could be persuaded. I think some of our mob could be persuaded too. He wants to get private investment into public services, new houses instead of lower rents. A boom for the property market and the second home owner."

"Not very socialist," observed Roberts.

"That's my point."

A few days later, Cranshaw met Fiona in an upmarket cafe on the south side of town.

"Little Fifi," he said. He said this even though she was in her fifties and he in his seventies. "So glad you decided to meet."

She fussed with her handbag and then sat down. Cranshaw signalled the waitress and ordered a pot of tea.

"Earl Grey alright?" he asked. Fiona nodded her assent.

"Why do I get the feeling, this is not just for old time's sake?" she asked.

"Because it isn't. Come on Fifi, what are you and your husband up to. You're meant to be retired."

"Up to? Don't know what you mean Gordie."

"Peter, quietly waving the flag for this Bland fellow. He's not doing that off his own bat."

Fiona sipped her tea and paused for a moment. "What do you think of Bland, his chances?" she said eventually.

"What do my friends back at the firm think of him you mean?"

"Yes."

"They are a little tired of the incumbents, but hardly ready to keep the red flag flying at this point. The fear is he's a friendly face on the same old monster. Do you know different?"

"We're not sure."

Cranshaw leaned back, narrowed his eyes, assessing her. "Well. I won't interfere just yet," he said, "unless one of you asks me to. Of course, if you think there is something I would LIKE to know .. for old time's sake, as you mentioned."

"Of course."

"And how are the rest of the family?"

"Philip is still a practitioner. We try to encourage him to open a private practice, but he insists on remaining content where he is."

"Some people are like that."

"Eustace in the civil service. Martha and Simone married. Andrew of course, with his job at the council, writing those articles that embarrass us."

"Let him. That sort of thing has helped us more than he realises. Gives us something to point at."

"And you?"

"Retired really of course, I keep my hand in mainly as something to do, since Elaine died."

Fiona smiled sympathetically. "I must call dad," she said, "remind him to go see you, although he doesn't get about as much as he used to."

"None of us do Fifi. That's the sad thing."

The next day, when Peter had driven into town, Fiona went into the garage, and from the glass jar of odds and ends they kept on the shelf in there, fished out the spare key to her husband's writing desk, the existence of which he remained blissfully ignorant. She went back inside and unlocked the desk and found the soft leather bound file that Eustace had brought up from London with him. Internal documents from the civil service. They were all but rearranging the desks in anticipation of Bland's appointment. The general feeling that:

'this is a man we can work with'. Copy of Eustace's retirement letter from the service. His appointment to Bland's staff. Eustace was right in his assumptions. She had underestimated him.

She met up with Andrew in a town centre cafe, this one decidedly more proletarian than the one in which she had met Cranshaw. There was only one kind of tea for a start, what the Americans would have called builder's tea. Andrew was eating toast.

"Going to tell me off again mother?" he asked, wiping the crumbs from his mouth with a paper napkin, then fiddling with his ponytail.

"I was planning to help you, if I can."

"How do you mean?" He was expectant all of a sudden. "You can loan me some money, after all?"

"Not that no. Look darling. I know you only write these terrible articles out of frustration. The job, it wasn't what you wanted. It's .. well, we don't know what you wanted really. We couldn't pay you to do nothing in the factory office forever."

"Unfair."

"But listen, you've heard of Bland. You and your friends at the Worker."

"A popinjay. They hate him. I just wrote an article calling him out."

"Don't print it."

"You always say that. But what would be so embarrassing about this one?"

"It wouldn't. Only for you, when he becomes head of the party."

"Head of the party ... how would you .." he paused. "Brother Eustace."

"Maybe."

"So that's .. " He leaned back, stared to one side, nodding, contemplating the matter.

"If you're the one who supports him, writes a conciliatory article, you might end up with a career after all, something good. And your boy Brandon, he's getting older now. Big school soon then college."

He thought about it for a while, his tongue rolling around his mouth.

"There is something you need to know also," he said, after a while.

"Oh really?" Fiona creased her brow.

"It's Uncle Anthony." Fiona's brow creased further. "He's been saying how father has started hanging round the pubs and such, getting involved in politics again. So, Anthony started talking to some friends of mine at the Worker, a lot of old scandal, about how father ripped off Anthony and Ursula's share of the family inheritance, just because they were illegitimate. Told my friends to publish that story.

Luckily, they thought to run it past me. They needn't do you know."

Fiona had gone pale slightly. The tale was grimy enough to scupper some of Peter's plans.

"It's true then?" said Andrew. "He waited until Anthony was away, then talked Grandma into signing over the paper mill to him. Sold it and used the money to bail out your parent's factory."

"Uncle Anthony is a drunkard and ne'er do well," she said. "Any money that family ever made came from his wife, cleaning and doing chores, while he took it straight out of her hands and into the pub. Same now with his children's wages."

"Doesn't stop the tale being true though, does it?"

"What else is he up to?"

"Can't say for sure. I think cousin Sylvester goes round there, maybe you could ask him."

Sylvester had been brought up by his grandmother Adelaide, ever since his mother Ursula had died of leukaemia. They lived together in a small terrace, the home of her former lover Eric McGonall, Anthony and Ursula's father. She had taken up with him following the death of her husband Martin Redgrave, Peter's father, from emphysema. He had been a hand in the paper mill her family owned, somewhat below her station, and even then, there had been questions about her mental acuity. Her father had died in the war and two years later her mother had run away to Scotland with a railwayman, leaving the business in her hands. She may have been depressed and unstable when she married Martin, who was frail and exempt from military service. His death from chest conditions, exacerbated by dust and fibres in the mill, seemed to come as little surprise anyway, and she moved in with Eric, a bookies runner and occasional asphalt spreader, without even bothering to marry a second time. This was a scandal and Peter suffered for it at school, snubbed by the teachers, teased and bullied by his peers. Anthony, on the contrary, grew up feral and had a gang prepared to fight anyone attempting to give him a hard time, while Ursula was by nature timid, eventually marrying a milliner who doted on her. When Eric, in the 1960s, drunkenly stole a car and got himself killed rolling it over during the subsequent police pursuit, Ade's mental problems came to the fore and that was when the fits started. Peter by then had left school and silently started distancing himself from the rest of the family, while at the same time assuming control of the business. During Eric and Ade's time together, the running of the mill had been left to a 'trusted' employee, who of course had been skimming the takings mercilessly. He had the man fired, which led to some aggravation and let it be known, in certain circles, that he regarded the business as more of an asset than an obligation. He worked on improving his social standing, playing against his mother's reputation: as a man of recalcitrant moral character, gaining access to the church and later, even better, the golf club and that was how he met Fiona Puesch. She was somewhat older than him and as things stood in those days, rather in danger of being 'left on the shelf'. Upon meeting, they recognised something in each other, that each could be the foil for the others ambitions, and this proved to be as solid a basis for attraction as anything else. Peter sold the mill to a developer who eventually knocked it down and built a supermarket, and with the money they bought their way into her parent's factory and then got married. This marriage seemed to erase and mitigate the worst of his family history, although later, a grudgeful ex-employee or unscrupulous competitor might conspire to bring up certain facts in anger. During all this time, Anthony had been happy to leave Peter in charge of family affairs as long as some small stipend found its way into his pocket and supplemented his income and Ursula was diffident enough to agree with him when he claimed that it was all for the best. It wasn't until he came back from the continent where he'd been attempting to sell fake watches, that Anthony discovered how the mill had been sold off and all the proceeds put into his brother's new business.

Now Sylvester was in Anthony's kitchen, sharing a meal of beans on toast with his Uncle's family: his wife Josie and two of the three children: Janice, who worked as a hairdresser, and John an apprentice joiner. The eldest Lisa had run away with a boyfriend to London two years ago. Janice's three year old boy Aaron was nearby clattering around with some plastic toys, while Anthony was washing down his beans with lager.

"Beans Sylvio," he said. "All we can bloody afford. What do you make of that?"

"You're not working?" asked Sylvester.

"Not if I can bloody help it no!" Anthony cried animatedly. "And anyway, what for? Knacker myself out for the sake of some tosspot manager's career! Or for the sake of the stockholders! Sod that. I'll stick with my cash in hand."

"What can you do though, if you've got a family to support?"

"They need warehousemen at the supermarket," said Josie quietly. "Just a few hours a day."

"And then they take it off your benefits. Don't be stupid woman .." She shied back from her comments immediately. "That reminds me," Anthony continued. "I saw that cow Fiona coming out of Sainsburys yesterday, full trolley, straight into their BMW. That's alright, isn't it?"

"Ade says that Uncle Peter helped you out, once you came back from Amsterdam."

"Helped me out?! Are you joking? Fucking paid me off he did. Fifty quid to stop me mouthing off about the five grand he owed me. Know where we'd be if we got our share? In a tasty fucking mansion instead of this dump. And listen, it wasn't just me they robbed, it was your mother too. A bit more money behind her she might have been able to look after herself."

"What difference would that have made? My father took care of her the best he could."

"And it broke his heart. Listen. If you were a proper man, you'd come with me to Uncle Pete's and give him what for. Kick up a stink. See if we can shake some money out of the bastard."

"I don't want their money."

"Don't want their money, eh? Well, let's see how life treats you. One day you're gonna need it, then I'll watch you eat those words. My family. They'd let me die like a dog before throwing me a crust" He mused for a while. "Who I really don't trust? That Andrew. His articles for The Worker, impress his socialist friends in the planning department. But he'll dance to daddy's tune if he gets a whiff of the old man's cash, I'll bet you ten to the dollar .. "

"I'm alright. I make enough as a mechanic to take care of me and Adie."

"I'm just trying to tell you. In this world it's the good ones that suffer and the bastards that get rich. And your grandmother, how do you think they treated her? Sold off what she had then shoved her into that pokey terrace. Now that Fiona talks of putting her in a loony bin so she doesn't embarrass them all."

"They better not."

"That's more like it. And what if they do? What do you reckon you can do about it, my brother gets his way?"

"What do you mean?"

"Cosying up to the Tories all his life. Now he's in the pubs talking about the workers struggle, about this Blunt .. Bland. What do you make of that?"

"I don't know."

"Me neither. But he's up to something."

When Sylvester got back to his grandmother's house, he was none too surprised to find Uncle Peter waiting for him, the BMW parked up outside the terrace. He swung his modified Ford Focus into the kerb so that the two cars were facing each other, headlamp to headlamp, then switched off the engine. They both got out of their cars at the same time and shook hands.

"Hello Uncle," said Sylvester. "You haven't been out this way for a while."

"No, I realised," said Peter, "thought I'd call in, see how the old gal was doing. How is she?"

"About the same. More fits. Phillip comes round to check on her and gives me a prescription for sedatives." He was taking some keys out of his trouser pocket and unlocking the door.

"Ah, that's a good boy."

"How are you?"

"We're doing fine, thanks for asking." They were in the hallway and could hear the television in the sitting room. Peter braced himself and strode in. It was indeed a poky room, the wallpaper twenty years old at least. His mother was sat in an upholstered armchair facing the television, which was showing some soap opera about doctors, but it couldn't be said she was watching it. She stared at some unseen point about a foot to the left. He went over and kissed her on the cheek. "Hello mother," he said softly, "it's Peter, how are you?"

Her eyes swivelled to look at him for a moment, and she smiled uncertainly, adjusted her false teeth with her tongue and went back to staring at the wall. Peter sighed. "How often is she like this?" he asked.

"Maybe four hours a day, then later she talks: about Eric mainly." Peter tried not to, but a trace of disdain swept over his face.

"Yes, " he said. "The good old days."

"Cup of tea?"

"Yes, I will, thanks." He followed Sylvester into the kitchen and they waited for the kettle to boil. "You've been seeing your Uncle Anthony," he observed.

Sylvester sagged slightly with relief, that they were getting to the point. "Yes, I have."

"He talks about me."

"A lot."

"I see. Well, he's been going through some hard times. It makes him resentful. In the future I might be in a position to help him more."

"Is that so."

"It is. In fact, I'm quite optimistic about the future. The problem is, the stuff he's been saying, it puts that in jeopardy."

"I think that's the point."

"You have to realise it's nonsense. Mother signed everything over to me because she saw I was the best person to handle it, that's all. And the paperwork backs that up, it ever comes to court."

The kettle was coming to a boil. Sylvester picked it up, flung two teabags into mugs and added the steaming water. "And why would it come to court?" he asked.

"He's been trying to work it into a scandal, get it in print, the Worker, do you know it?" Sylvester shrugged. "No, I guess you wouldn't .. the point is they ran it past my son Andrew, who put a block on it .. but if, IF, I told him to go ahead and publish .. it might scupper some of my plans, might, but the defamation suit I could launch would leave Anthony dodging bailiffs the rest of his life." Peter laughed suddenly. "But of course, I'd rather it didn't come to that."

"Of course." Sylvester looked out of the window and sipped his tea.

Peter took a brown envelope out of his coat pocket. "There's a grand there," he said. "It's all we can spare right now, but if things go well for us .. we might be in a position to help him some more."

"If he keeps his mouth shut."

"If he keeps his mouth shut, that's a precondition. I'd like you to take it to him, explain things. Take a hundred for yourself if you need to."

"I'll see what he says. If he doesn't agree, I'll bring back the full amount."

Peter shrugged. "That's up to you," he said, putting the envelope down on the kitchen counter. He took his mug of tea with him back into the sitting room, where the television was still blaring, this time an advertisement for a pension plan. He looked at the old wallpaper, the tufted maroon carpet, the green tile mantelpiece, upon which rested a brass clock, and the framed sampler above it - God Bless This House. The curtains were heavy, tan coloured, and grey light filtered through the net blinds. Behind Adelaide's armchair was a 1960s wall unit which complemented the other bits of furniture scattered about - a veneered coffee table and a two seater settee. Upon it were arranged various momentos that she was in the habit of examining during the early hours of the morning: pewterware, pottery animals, framed black and white photos - her with him as a young boy in shorts and a smudge of dirt on his cheek, sitting on the doorstep of the old house, two of her with Eric, on the promenade at the seaside, a picnic out in the countryside somewhere. None of his father. He sensed that Sylvester had followed him into the room.

"You know the thing about the good old days," he said. "They were wretched. Now they've been built over, the same way they built that supermarket over our mill. You walk past now, it's like nothing else was ever there."

Sylvester didn't reply. He went over to the unit, found Adie's cigarettes and put them down on the table next to her so they nestled against the glass ashtray.

"I feel like a double agent," said Andrew to Vollet, and there was indeed something about their meeting, in the bandstand of the local park, reminiscent of a spy movie or the clandestine rendezvous of illicit lovers. It was a damp, chill day, just a few dog walkers and duck feeders around.

"I was surprised by your article that's all," said Vollet. "The Case for Moderation: you can't make change if you don't win elections."

"You do read The Worker then?"

"Somebody has to."

Andrew chuckled.

"How did it go down with your colleagues?"

"Not very well. There's many calling me a sellout. Say I'm working for my father."

"Are you?"

"No, that's your job."

Vollet chuckled this time. "He wants the Gazette to push Bland, that's true. I have the same kind of problem as you though. My investors say I'm trying to stab them in the back, playing pinko politics."

"God forbid a newspaper should reflect the interests of its readers."

"That's not their job at all, no. So .. I take it you're banking on Bland winning the leadership contest."

"He has a good chance don't you think? And then to take on your mob in the elections."

"He has a chance. And it might not be disagreeable, entirely."

"So, you are going to push him?"

Vollet demurred. "I was thinking more along the lines of a small thinkpiece .. how I chanced upon an article in The Worker - that irredeemable hotbed of radicalism - calling for compromise, the winds of change, well I never .. something along those lines. Test the waters with the readership."

"So, we are starting to row our boats in accord. It's very touching isn't it," said Andrew with a slight sneer.

"You've said some unkind things about me .. in print .. but I'm a forgiving sort of fellow. You learn to be, when you're a professional."

Andrew laughed. "Let's not get above ourselves," he said. "You run the local rag and I contribute to a party financed press."

"Little acorns," said Vollet. "Little acorns."

2. To the victor the spoils

"Come in brother," said Eustace, "I was expecting you." He stepped back to allow Andrew inside his Battersea apartment. It was formal inside, austere, more like an office than a living space.

"So," said Andrew, "you did alright for yourself. Backed the right horse."

Eustace nodded with a slight trace of smugness. "And you. Thanks to mother. They reprinted some of your articles as part of the election campaign."

"Yes, but it hasn't really led anywhere has it."

"Give it time. I'll keep my eye out for something .. a position. But in the meantime, you mustn't dance attendance upon me, it looks bad. Stay low down here and I'll let you know when something suitable crops up."

"I put Brandon into that private school."

"Oh, really brother, not the local comprehensive?"

"Angela insisted, but financially .."

"I'll cover the fees for the first year. But consider that a loan."

"Thank you."

"And how are you settling in?"

"We're in Hammersmith."

"Not a bad district."

"If you like being near to the ringroad and the hospital, with the emergency ambulances blaring past with their sirens all night, waking up your one year old daughter who starts crying again, yes it's fine."

"The move to London should always be an adventure."

"But you will look for something."

"As I promised."

There was a bit more chit chat and then, the meeting more or less over, he returned by cab to the apartment they were renting. It was just off the Broadway, a shabby one bedroom affair and Angela was boiling pasta while their one year old Claudia slept, mercifully, in the crib.

"How did it go?" she asked, looking tired.

Andrew went over to the crib, looked down at Claudia and smiled sentimentally.

"Says he'll keep an eye out," he replied, after a moment.

"That's all?"

"For now, he has to be prudent."

"Prudent? After those articles you wrote. Why can't he get you a place on the PR team, like we talked about?"

"Has to be careful apparently. Him and the press secretary don't exactly see eye to eye."

"We sold up the house to come here, he knows that, that it's a gamble for us? To be renting this place like a pair of students again."

"He's working on something. Slow and steady, that's my brother. Reliable though, he won't let us down." At least, I hope he won't, thought Andrew, looking round at the place with its thin carpet and its radiators and mottled peuce wallpaper. It was like being a student again - they'd been married with a kid, Brandon, when they'd gone down to Bristol together, about the only ones there who were, using their parents' money to support themselves. Not that he'd told the other students that, instead inventing some ludicrous story about being 'cut off' by Angela's capitalist parents and joining Clause Four. In fact, it was his 'tip off' that several nationalist conservative politicians were due to speak at the Student Union that led to the violent campus protests of 87, and his coverage of the event in the student journal Bacchus, that led to him writing for the Worker .. it was only a job at the end of it all that failed to materialise, nothing seemed quite right to him and he'd taken on the role at his parent's factory, then the one at the council, all the while waiting for something else ...

Angela turned back to attend to the pan which was bubbling over and he unfolded the newspaper he'd bought from the newsagents, sat down on the wooden frame, green cushioned armchair that had come with the place and started to peruse the job advertisements, just in case. Outside, down in the street, an ambulance raced past, sirens high pitch and Claudia woke up and started to screech and wail. He sighed, looked at Angela, who obstinately remained with the pasta working on a tomato sauce, so he got up and went over to the crib himself and picked the child up, trying to calm her.

So, it was a relief when he was called to Eustace's apartments for a second time. This was a month later, and he had spent the meantime visiting the museums, bothering Eustace with phone calls and messages, trying to track down some old student friends who had moved to the city, and very tentatively circling job advertisements. He arrived there in a state of anticipation, hopping from one foot to the other as he waited outside the building to be buzzed in. It was cold, early winter. The apartment faced onto the park, the bare trees of which shivered in the crisp air. Eventually the buzzer sounded and he pushed open the double doors, entered the hallway and made his way up the staircase to the second floor. The door to his brother's flat had been left open and he walked inside to where Eustace was standing over his black desk holding a document.

"Here you are," he said. "I told you I'd find something." Andrew went over and tried not to snatch the papers out of his brother's hand. He read them carefully. The expression of disappointment slid down his face like rainwater pushing grime down a window for it to settle against the sill. 'Deputy Officer for Planning and Administration in the Borough of Hackney' he read. Eustace monitored his brother's reaction carefully. "Yes, you were expecting something rather grand," he said. "But I'm afraid you'll have to learn to stoop if you want to pick up a fortune. Patience too. If we gave everyone what they asked for straight away, the coffers would soon be empty and that's the way of it."

Andrew remained silent. He was actually pale, quite horrified. It was but a step up from his previous job. Eustace tried a calmer tone of voice.

"We recognise both your qualities and ambitions. We intend also, to choose our friends from the most rapacious, but you have to wait. In the meantime, this position is appropriate to your experience."

Andrew continued to look glum. Eustace moved closer, gripped the top of the document and physically lowered it so he could look into his brother's eyes.

"Take it," he said. "All you have to do is keep your eyes and ears open if money is what you're after. The only thing you need to avoid is a scandal. That is what we won't tolerate."

Andrew gradually came out of his stupor. He nodded slowly, revived by the hint of potential loot. "Okay," he said eventually. "If that's the way you want to play it."

"It is. And there's one other thing you might want to consider - taking your wife's surname. It would make it less easy for people to associate the pair of us."

"Andrew Sykes? God no, I sound like a geography teacher."

"Some variation thereof .. Sacks."

"Andrew Sacks .. yes that will do it: sacks of cash, sacks of opportunity, the sack of Rome. It inspires confidence."

Eustace snorted, but he was amused. "Yes," he said. "You could be a millionaire or a criminal. One day perhaps, both."

Opportunity did not come knocking until two years later, during which time Andrew led the life of the city's countless clerks and office workers: commuting on the tube, eating prepacked sandwiches, Friday night drinks at the pub near to the office. But working on hints from Eustace, asking the right innocuous questions to the right people in the right departments, he was able to establish a very clear notion of which impoverished neighbourhoods were scheduled to receive regeneration grants under the newly elected regime. The issue then was the necessary finance to take advantage of such knowledge. He met Eustace discreetly in one of those genteel pubs that furnish the corners of Chelsea and Kensington, not too far from Battersea, across the pink and green Albert bridge. They settled into one of the snugs, nursing their pints of Guinness.

"No, no," said Eustace, "it's quite out of the question for any money to come from me, or my acquaintances. We have to appear squeaky clean."

"Then who? Point me in the direction of a name."

Eustace made a display of pondering the matter. "Have you seen our sister since you moved to London," he said eventually.

"Simone? She came to see us when we first moved here, but no, not much since. Actually, Angela sees more of her than me .. she's an admirer. Personally, I can't make out what it is that she does, since the divorce. Picked up some of her husband's legal work as I understand."

Eustace seemed privately amused, which was something he'd made rather a habit of. "Oh, it's a lot more arcane than that," he said. "Although legalities are involved sometimes. She matches up people's problems, is the best way I can describe it."

The shop from which Simone ostensibly conducted her business was not too much of a walk from Chelsea as it so happened, a stroll down the Kings Road with the Thames running adjacent, passed the Hammersmith bridge this time, more functional than the Albert in yellow and maroon paint, towards the district known as Worlds End. The expensive boutiques of the Kings Road here gave way to something less ostentatious: electrical goods outlets and betting shops and the vintage store that his sister 'ran', if you made it through the front door - for it rarely seemed to be trading - was little more than a front for the real business being conducted in the office upstairs. Here there was an old wooden desk, a vinyl bound swivel chair, piles and boxes of paper and documents, and a computer which was put into use only with reluctance and its hard drive regularly exchanged. His sister, after bolting the front door, unlocking the door that led to the staircase connecting the two floors, and leading him up to the office, pulled up a tubular art deco stool for him to sit on, and parked herself in the vinyl chair on the opposite side of the desk. She wore a masculine tweed business suit, brogues, and was always seen with her hair pulled back into a tight bun. This, altogether with her demeanour, made her seem older, or perhaps more mature, than her thirty two years.

"What you need is a divorce," she said. "Eustace agrees."

"A divorce," he laughed, "why?"

"Then you could remarry. There's certain overseas businessmen, would pay a significant amount of money to have a member of their family gain legal residency here. It would open a lot of financial doors for them."

"I couldn't. I've no reason for a divorce."

"God almighty. A reason can always be found for a divorce. We're hardly living in a papacy."

"Angela .. I couldn't even begin to broach the subject .."

"I can do that for you. It just needs to be put the right way, with the right sort of divorce settlement. It will mean a percentage of your earnings going to her ad infinitum, thirty percent I believe I can negotiate, so you have to consider - what return on your investments you're really expecting."

"Considerable I think."

"So, she might agree. And it only has to be a divorce in name. Relations can continue, unofficially."

"The marriage would be a sham?"

"It can be as much of a sham as you want it to be. That's between you and the family."

He hesitated. It didn't feel right.

"Hurts your sensibilities brother?"

"I just can't imagine Angela agreeing."

Simone laughed. "Then you don't understand her. But then what men do? Believe me, you need to put aside your ego here. I can get you a lot of investment without the usual strings or questions."

"The family, what are they like?"

"Romanian or something. Anyway, they want to get into property in London but they need someone with residency. That's why I put you together, this works out for all concerned."

"Yes." Andrew bit his lip. His conscience bothered him somewhat, and events felt rather surreal. But perhaps that was the illusion. Breaking through the glass wall of your reality so far, that was how you moved forward.

"I don't like it exactly no," said Angela. They were sat in Moretti's, a good restaurant near the South Bank. Andrew toyed with his pasta. Through the glass, across the water, was the monolithic arts centre.

"I've met her and she's shallow," he said. "She just wants to come to London and buy dresses really."

"She's pretty?"

"Yes, but I can't see her throwing herself at me, she's about three inches taller for a start. And I can't afford to upset her uncle by making it complicated. It's a practical arrangement that's all. One that benefits everyone."

"Thirty percent?"

"Yes."

"How much are you planning to make exactly? I mean, it's not like you never hinted at your plans. I just thought, you know, a mortgage and we invest in one or two properties. Where we know the prices are going to go up."

"So did I, until I saw the extent of it, the redevelopment."

"A lot?"

"All across the East End. The way I see it. You used to need poor people in the middle of the city, yes? To do the work. Not anymore. They can live right on the edge where there's fucking nothing and travel in. Or better, move the industry out there too. Then in the middle, where there's a point for a rich bastard to move to London, lots of lovely empty waterfront. The docks are fucked. They're building new roll on roll off facilities nearer to the estuary where they can get the massive ships in, a whole island. That's where the work is going to be. The only proletariat they're going to need around Hackney are cleaners and waiters."

"So how much are you going to buy?"

"As much as I can, but it has to be through a second party. Simone's sorting that out for me."

Angela sipped some wine and looked at the new potatoes and green beans on her plate. It occurred to her that if Andrew was going to end up in jail, a divorce might be prudent anyway. "The strange thing is," she said, "if I agree, we won't see in the new year together. A fresh millennium and we'll be separate, for appearances sake."

Andrew looked up shocked. It wasn't something he'd really thought about. As it was, he spent new year's eve alone in a hotel room, watching the fireworks explode over the Millenium Dome at Greenwich docks and listening to the distant cheers as the glittering reflections sparkled on the water.

 As stated, it was necessary for Andrew Sacks to purchase his first properties through an intermediary, to avoid charges of corruption and the related scandal that his brother had warned him against. This was a dubious letting agent by the name of Larson, located for him by his sister, who was 'loaned' the money by his new spouse's uncle Mr. Cassel. They had chosen together a squalid street of red brick terraces, all privately owned and out of the hands of the council but located in a district marked for future redevelopment. Larson bought up one or two that were on the market, and offered what seemed like outrageous prices to those landlords who were open to offers. Then, for those which were let to tenants he raised the rents, to such an extent that after two years, none of the original occupants - low paid and unemployed - were able to remain. Indeed no one who could have afforded the new rents and was of sensible mind would have chosen to live there. It seemed then that Mr Cassel was able to find plenty of friends willing to live, or pretend to live, in the properties, all of whose rent was actually paid by Mr Cassel himself. When the developers finally arrived and put in a purchase order, the 'value' of these buildings had increased fivefold and with the money from the sale Larson was able to repay back his loan with interest. With the additional profit he'd made he set up a new business - a consultancy for construction firms , advising them on how to land some of the new contracts by promising a token amount of 'social housing'. Andrew was appointed its executive manager, on a significant salary also paid for out of the profits. It was important, he said, that the firm sounded impartial and unconnected to the building industry, so they gave it a name that made it sound more like a charity - ShelterForPeople. Then released from the restrictions of his council role, Andrew was free to buy up properties and land all across the East End, assets whose value all increased massively as the old buildings were demolished and the sleek waterfront apartment blocks went up and financiers and wealthy professionals moved in. Mr Cassel too invested his acquaintance's money in these new communities, buying up property through a company set up in his niece's name. Everybody was starting to do remarkably well.

The limousine drove Brandon from his boarding school to his father's new flat on the docks. It was part of a magnificent structure in glass and steel, tapered at one end in the manner of a cruise ship. They entered through a security gate and slid through the clipped landscaped surroundings, down a ramp to the underground carpark. Then he accompanied the chauffeur to an elevator which brought them up to a small lobby and the chauffeur keyed Brandon into the apartment. It was massive. The sitting room alone had the square meterage of the suburban house he vaguely remembered living in as a child. One glass wall looked out over the Thames and the crowded city beyond. The floor was laminated in oak with a large Persian rug in the centre and the room furnished with a carefully selected mixture of Eames and Starck furniture. A Basquiat style painting dominated one wall. The chauffeur asked him if he wouldn't mind waiting, bowed, and left him to his own devices. Brandon didn't mind waiting at all. He went over to a glass topped table and found the remote control. He played with the buttons - various lights went on and off, the television appeared, the stereo started playing some kind of east european hip hop ... then the door reopened and Renata walked into the room, taking off her chequered riding cap and pink stole and casting them onto a nearby sofa. She wore a gold satin blouse with outsize buttons and sleeves that collected and puffed above the elbow, cropped trousers with pleats and expensive limited edition Adidas in herringbone tweed. As an ensemble it was crass and outrageous and mesmerising. Brandon stared, as he might have done if a unicorn had trotted into the room.

Renata stared back. "So, you're Brandon are you?" she asked. He nodded. "Well, I'm your new step mother I'm afraid - I suspect I should have been here to meet you but I got held up at my stylists. If Andrew stops by it might only be for dinner so we have to start getting used to each other. I don't know if I'm expected to be a mother exactly, but I want to be kind. That is what I kept saying to Hochi."

"How old are you?" asked Brandon.

"What a question to ask!" Renata exclaimed. "Not that I mind really. I am 23."

"I am 16," Brandon said. "We could actually be brother and sister."

She didn't seem to hear but walked to stand in front of a freestanding oval mirror in the corner of the room. "What do you think of this outfit?" she asked. "There is something missing isn't there." She twisted her lip, sincerely pained, anxious. She turned to face Brandon. "There is isn't there? Something gone!"

Brandon felt a desperate sudden need to assuage her anxiety. "A necklace," he said. "Something big, statement."

She slapped her palms to her cheeks and squealed. "YES!" she exclaimed. "That's right. A cross!" She turned to the mirror again. "A big cross, in something lurid - orange neon. YES! darling darling." She rushed over and kissed him on both cheeks. "Well, we are going to get on. I think thats obvious, but ... grow out that awful British public school haircut won't you, pleassse ..."

Brandon nodded his agreement. What else could he do?

By this time Andrews' early affiliation with the party had been remembered and his newfound experience of dealing with developers appreciated and he was put on a number of government quangos and committees. This was highly valued by his friends in the construction industry, and they were willing to pay increasingly high consultation fees on the condition that he push one agenda - that the lack of affordable housing never be made the fault of the property market and the solution always be to build more houses. As a reward for his good work, he was introduced to a stockbroker by the name of Bertrand St Claire and together they set up the Vauxhall Credit Agency, which lent money to struggling homeowners using half their mortgage as security. These mortgages were then jumbled together and sold on to speculators who traded with them on the market. He remembered one night, in order to make the securities look older and more respectable, they had taken them out to one of his building sites and trampled them in the dust, the way a forger might age a document with tea leaves. And all this time he was lauded by his peers as a champion of the socially deprived and underprivileged, a fiction that at moments he half believed.

"Your darling wife is in the gossip columns again," said Angela. They were sat in the garden of her Suffolk cottage, watching their daughter and her friend play with some dolls and a teaset on the lawn.

"Oh god," groaned Andrew, "who is it this time?"

"Let's see," Angela scrolled down the pages of her laptop. "Spotted coming out of some club called Vortex with a fellow name of Zack. Used to be in a boyband apparently but now describes himself as a singer-songwriter. His latest song 'Look at Me' is in the charts. Impressive."

"Brandon?"

"Not too far behind .. a weathergirl turned aspiring actress. Nice. You'd like her."

Andrew grimaced.

"I'd say there's grounds for divorce, you ever wanted to find it."

"I can't yet. Cassal says at least three more years, to make the citizenship claim rock solid. Are you ... with anyone?"

"There's a chap. Architect. How about you?"

"An intern I keep sequestered in Bayswater. That's all."

"Hmm. It was worth it, wasn't it? We jumped quite far."

"I think it was worth it. As long as you're settled and Claudia does okay."

"She asks about you of course. Loves it when you visit. I have her enrolled at St. Lukes."

"Ah, that's good." He looked over. Claudia noticed him watching and cried out, "Daddy, daddy, Maisie won't play fair. Look!" She stood up to kick over the teapots.

"Claudia, NO!" shouted Angela. Andrew sighed and went to sort out the mess. He picked up Claudia and rubbed her head under his chin. "Don't be silly now," he murmured, "behave for your old man."

"That's her," said Brandon. His hair was longer now, curling to his shoulders. "Laura she's called." They were in a cab parked across from the apartment in Bayswater, watching the intern leave and set off towards Whitehall.

"You think she's pretty?" asked Renata.

"Attractive in a dull and efficient way, why do you care?"

"I don't know, I just noticed your father's been paying more of my bills lately. Do you like the bracelet he bought me, it's Cartier." She held up her arm so they could see the sapphires sparkle in the watery yellow autumn light that perforated the cab's rear window. Outside the London plane trees were hanging on to the last of their leaves.

"So, he buys you jewellery and pays her rent. He must be doing well."

"You swine." She punched his arm.

Brandon looked sideways to evaluate her. It was now four years since their first meeting and since dropping out of St Martins college he was really doing nothing apart from contemplating the vague idea of having a fashion brand. "You're not actually jealous, are you?"

She thought about it then shook her head. "Bored." She laid her head back against the cab seat, and said through gritted teeth, "somehow I am bored to death."

"It's your nerves maybe."

"Yes," she retorted sarcastically, "it's my nerves."

"If this is a confession, is it going to be a long one?"

"Oh, what do you know?"

"Well, you can hardly complain. You spend tens of thousands of pounds a year on your wardrobe, you have an apartment and now a country house, you can indulge yourself in whatever project you want, and your latest outfit pushes the war off the front page of the dailies. There are men who would drop a grand just to kiss your feet. Is it not so?"

"I suppose so."

"And yet you feel bored. What is it? What's the problem?"

"I want something else."

"Something else! What?"

"That's the problem. I don't know." Brandon winced, irritated. He tapped on the partition of the cab and they started to move.

"I'm just sick of the parties and premieres, they're just the same thing" she continued. "And the men. The men are unbearable."

"Really?" Brandon laughed. "I can't say I noticed you avoiding them."

"Yes, you are unbearable. I don't say that about you, you're too young. But if you knew how your father .. wearied me, and all those others too. If I'm jealous of that Laura, it's because .. she has her own life. Something less craven."

Brandon scoffed. Looked out of the window as they passed Hyde Park, at the loitering people, the ones on bikes, the joggers and dog walkers. "And you think half her career isn't going to be built on shagging my father," he said. "Come on, Rena." The cab passed among the extravagant townhouses of Mayfair, then slowed down as it reached Covent Garden, moving in steady lurches through the throngs of tourists, then driving through the once notorious slums of Whitechapel, a crowded Bangladeshi district now with the odd remnant of previous communities poking through like an archeological artefact - a pre-war pub or a Chinese grocery. Eventually they arrived outside the gates of their newly constructed, private closed community, and Renata got out while Brandon dealt with the fare. He had a separate apartment here now, in a separate building, and sometimes when she heard a cab in the early morning, she could part the blinds to see him spill out of its rear doors with a party of friends or a woman he'd picked up. Architectural showpieces littered the waterfront and it was quiet, apart from the caw of gulls, drifting between the buildings as though they were isolated coastal tors, looking in vain for a place to land. The streets around them were empty, devoid apart from the thrum now and again of a passing sports car. A cafe down the road had two customers sat outside on wrought iron chairs, nibbling on bagels and cappuccino.

"You notice what is strange?" she asked, as Brandon came and stood by her side.

"Apart from your mood. No," he said, "what is it that's so strange."

"You don't hear any children. In the streets. Never. This place is sterile."

"You'll be better when we get to the country."

"That reminds me, the Morrison's are visiting. Your father wants you to dress up and pay attention to Louise."

"Christ, what a drag. I have this theory .. a marriage to someone you find tedious will be preferable to courting them. You'll come and save me won't you, my darling mother?"

"Of course. There are times you know, when I think you'd prefer to be dating me." They looked at each other for a moment then, before going inside to dress for the country.

It was a restored 17th century country house with forty acres of land on the outskirts of an Oxfordshire village that had long since ceased to be rural and become the haunt of retired bankers and wealthy professionals. As such, it many times resembled a stage set more than a community, the backdrop for some provincial farce in which the postmistress is found strangled with baling wire but no one is really affected and Inspector McDermot steps in to work his way through a clockwork plot. By the time they arrived, a variety of cars were parked on the drive outside. The chauffeur let them out of the car and went to the converted stables to smoke, exchange gossip and play cards and otherwise wile away the evening with his fellow drivers. Brandon and Renata were shown straight into the dining room by the rented valet. It was an expansive room lit by a large gilt chandelier that hung over the long wooden table, now covered with fine linen tablecloths trimmed with lace and laden with antique silverware and crystal cut glass in preparation for the meal. The walls were decorated in solemn green wallpaper patterned with gold chevrons and plaited borders, and a variety of 18th century landscape paintings in ornate frames, while the floor, door frames, ceiling and Revival furniture were all dark heavy oak, the antique effect broken up with red velvet sashes and drapes. The rest of the guests were already present - Andrew, Simone - who he had placed next to the exit doors in the 'ejector seat' location in between two contractors - and the Morrisons - the widower Harley and his daughter Louise, and around twenty other personages of various backgrounds and influence, the gentlemen in formal dinner dress and the ladies in couture dresses or carefully chosen designer ensembles.

Conversation halted as the pair entered the room. Brandon was dressed in a silver grey Brooks Brothers suit, with red and white Oxford plimsolls and a ruffled lavender shirt with a lily in the buttonhole, while Renata wore a tweed riding jacket in marmalade orange and apple green stripes that flared at the hip, with a floral blouse underneath and then a short corded skirt that hung over her paisley jodhpurs and this was all set off by her silver suede, fringed boots. Most of the gentlemen present murmured and rose to their feet. There was even scattered applause. Renata bowed, blushing ironically, then sat down near Andrew opposite the Harwells, while Brandon took his place with the 'younger set'. Mrs Harwell, the wife of the pharmaceutical director, openly admired Renata's bracelet, a circlet of alternating diamond and opal studded squares that peered out modestly from under her sleeve.

"That's the Tiffany isn't it, from the Spencer auction?" she said, then turned to Andrew. "Really Andrew, you are a superb husband, I should borrow you for a while." Andrew bowed politely. Then the soup tureen was brought in by the hired butler and carefully ladled into the guest's bowls.

"So," said Mr. Noyes, the Minister of Transport, "we do not have the pleasure of your brother's company tonight?"

"No," said Andrew. "He had to return to Brussels. His secretary sends his regrets."

"Yes, he's on the Commission now. Well, he's a talented man. Personally, I've always been grateful to him."

"The building loans," said Ms Roche, an investment banker for Stonewall and Jackson, "such a fine piece of engineering, a remarkable financial manoeuvre .."

" ..the lad pulled over of course, but it wasn't just her tyres he ended up pumping if you get my drift.." said Brandon, and there was a sharp peal of laughter from Louise at the far end of the table.

Andrew tried to mask his irritation and turn his attention back to Roche. "You can say what you like about the new developments," she was saying, "but they've brought money into London - financiers, investors actually want to live here."

"Well," said Andrew, "there are outside parties who have brought a lot of devotion to the work," and here he raised a wine glass to the two contractors - Briers and Connolly. Briers broke off from his conversation about soccer with Simone to shrug modestly, but Connolly stated, "it brought a lot of work to a lot of honest tradesmen. A real windfall for the working man."

"Not to mention the culture the developments bring to downtrodden areas," said Noyes, "the galleries and so forth."

"And as for the cost," said Mr Harwell, "our children can pay." There was a murmur of assent.

"I am a landlord myself," said Greaves the minister for Kensington, "and when I do up a flat I raise the rent. It's as simple as that."

"Very pithy," said the press baron Dewpepper, who was seated near to Andrew, "I might print that one tomorrow."

Briers at last broke into the conversation. "There's a lot of us managed to line our pockets," he said. "Things always look good when you're making money, if you ask me."

That abrupt comment brought an awkward lull of silence to the table.

"So you're saying you'd move Orlando into midfield?" Simone asked Briers, and the conversations suddenly jumpstarted again, while the butler and catering staff began clearing the soup dishes, and more wine was poured, and then the meat and fish dishes brought in. Renata was visibly bored, distracted, while Brandon and Louise were discussing the various outfits that had been worn to some film premiere the other week. "No," Brandon was saying, "it was the Gaultier but in blue .."

"The forthcoming elections," Andrew said to Noyes, "how are they looking?"

"Well, the war has had an impact," Noyes replied, "it's no good pretending it hasn't."

"Ohhhhh pleassse darling," Renata intoned suddenly to her husband, "Have some compassion and don't start on dreadful politics. Have mercy on us."

Noyes laughed. "She's right of course." He paused then said, "Did you really meet John Alton?" Renata nodded and said, "Tedious and irritating, more so than his music."

"No!... flamboyant surely. But then I suppose you prefer some of those rappers. There was one wanted you to be in his video wasn't there?"

Renata smirked. "I should have .. for what he was offering, but it would not have been quite respectable, you know?" Around them was talk of the West End theatre, horses, investments. Eventually, after dessert and more wine the guests began to quieten down. Cigars came out and there was talk of retiring to the drawing room. Only Brandon and Louise and some of the younger set were still animated, him telling a story that involved him walking his finger across the table and some of the others laughing. Renata stood up sharply and left the table and one by one the rest followed, swaying drunkenly. In the drawing room it was informal with mismatched settees, armchairs and divans settled around a marble fireplace and the dark prussian blue walls lightened by paintings of sailing ships or horse races. People settled into small groups and there was brandy and smoking and murmured gossip - the indiscretions of minor royals, hushed scandal that never made the papers. Simone was muttering to Greaves something about the Philippines. Desperate for air, Brandon found himself out on the veranda with a young marketing executive he'd brought by the name of Patel, smoking a discreet spliff.

"What's the matter with her anyway?" Patel was saying. "When I saw her last week, we got on fine, but now she just acts like she doesn't want to know. I don't even know what I've done wrong. Can you talk to her, Brandon: tell her that I'm suffering?"

"No one can talk to her when she's in this sort of mood. You'll have to figure it out yourself."

"You know I'm your friend Brandie, I've just been waiting for the chance to prove it. Do this for me please, I'm so miserable."

Brandon leant on the stone balustrade and sighed. "I can try," he said eventually. "But I can't promise anything. Most likely she'll just tell me not to interfere."

Patel cheered up and clapped Brandon on the back. "That's all I ask Brandie," he said, "just give it the old college try."

They returned to the drawing room. "It helps to be blaise," Brandon was saying. "That's generally how she likes it." He looked around for Renata but she was absent, so he excused himself and searched around until he found her in a small apartment in the east wing. It was decorated with yellow satin curtains that reflected light off the chandelier and were tied back with pale blue sashes, daisy patterned to match the wallpaper, an ebony piano, two display cabinets containing a variety of porcelain figurines, a dark black woollen carpet flecked with green, gold and pink and a Louis 14th table supporting an antique Chinese vase decorated with a delicately sketched river scene in blue and holding a bouquet of lilies and irises. The small couches and settees were upholstered in crushed orange velvet and the cushions were patterned with unfolding pink tulips. The french window was open to the conservatory and dead leaves had blown in to lie at Renata's feet as she stared out past its ferns and citrus trees, out through the glass at the evening sky. She must have seen him enter, as a reflection.

"So, your task wasn't so difficult after all," she said.

"I don't understand you," said Brandon.

"You and Louise, you didn't waste any time."

Brandon started to laugh. "Ah yes, we were telling stories. She's very funny. More like a bloke really."

Renata pursed her face.

"You don't think we were playing footsie, do you? If we are going to be married, we might as well save that sort of thing for later. Anyway, I have something more important to tell you. Listen. Patel is miserable, and I know it's not really my business but it wouldn't hurt me to impress him somehow."

Renata just turned and stared at him, in a disconcerting manner.

"Is there anything you'd like me to say?" asked Brandon

"Tell him that he bores me," said Renata. Then she walked back towards the drawing room. Left on his own for the moment, Brandon's gaze settled on the dead leaves, then he shrugged and followed her. Most of the older guests were getting ready to leave. It was irritating, but maybe he could fix Patel up with someone else.

Two weeks later Brandon and Renata ran into each other at a private party occurring in a trendy north London discotheque. Some weird angular techno was playing as small groups made tentative moves on the dancefloor and the people nearby drank and gossiped loudly. It was dark inside, lit only by screens of green and purple neon. Brandon had found himself among the cast of a popular youth based soap opera and had his arm placed optimistically around one of the actresses. They were both high, the production assistant having supplied the crew with a small plastic sachet of ecstacy, and they alternated between talking animatedly and necking. As they broke off from a kiss Brandon looked over suddenly to see Renata was there, watching him from the top of two low steps that led down to the antechamber he and the thespians were occupying. Her right half was illuminated bright lime green by the neon panel next to her, while her left half was in shadow. She was wearing a white pvc trouser suit dotted with fluorescent polka dots, the sleeves and legs cut short and strapless heels, accompanied by an Italian riding cap and a bewildering array of bangles and pink hoop glitter filled earrings. She turned and went over to the bar and so Brandon extricated himself from the actress and walked over to stand beside her. She was finishing a double vodka and cranberry. They leant against the brightly lit perspex counter, which cast pink light upwards against their faces. The music whined behind them.

"It's so stupid," she said. She was crying.

He stared: his drugged mind floating in a thin pleasant space. He was still aroused from his foreplay with the actress and now his eyes wandered up and down Renata's costume.

"I have a hotel," he said. "Overlooking Westminster."

She nodded glumly, but with a strange smile of disdain curling up her lip on one side. She got her coat from the cloakroom, synthetic tiger fur with a high padded collar and they took a cab over to the hotel.

"So, who invited you?" he asked.

"Schaffer."

"The producer?"

"Yes." She looked out of the window at the night lights of the city as they slipped by, reflections sliding against the car window, all streetlamps and takeaways at this time, an all night grocery. "Wants me to do a programme, something to do with music."

"All these offers. You can take one of them you know. You'd be great."

"None of them are serious you notice. They expect me to caper about and play the giddy goat."

He looked at the taxi roof exasperated and with the serotonin rush pummeling through his body not up to much critical thinking beside.

"You could do what you want and you'd be great at it, that's all I know."

They did not say much else until they got to the hotel, crossing the marble lobby to get in the elevator.

"Did you see the concierge?" said Brandon grinning. "I bet he thought you were an escort."

She looked at him frankly then without blinking. "And if I was," she said. "What would you pay me to do?" The atmosphere in the elevator tightened up like a knot had been twisted and then he leaned over her and pressed the hold button and kissed her fiercely pushing his hand down the front of her trousers into her underwear feeling her snatch, then biting her chin, brought it out and tried to undo the zip on her top to get at her breasts but she caught his hand and pulled back and looked at him while he panted.

"Wait," she said.

He shook his head and pressed in again, trying with the other hand but she bent his arm around backwards rotating him until the pain caused him to stop and she brought up her leg to rub it slowly against his stiffening groin, then pressed the button to restart the lift.

"Do as you're told," she said.

Afterwards they were in the hotel room with the sheets still tied to the bedposts. The curtains were apart and you could see the Abbey's dome as a shadowy mass against the dull early morning sky. Brandon was sat naked on a towel covered chair drinking champagne while Renata, in her coat, did a line of cocaine off the dresser top. His mind was very hollow and abstract and he felt sated.

"Well," he said, "I suppose that was bound to happen sooner or later." He had the vague feeling he should be embarrassed but it didn't feel relevant. "What do you think about it?" he asked.

She snorted a couple of times and looked out of the window. "It's ridiculous of course," she said. She felt like crying in some way but was trembling with delight too. It was hard to make sense of her feelings except that she hoped it would rain. That would be good to watch, a grey rain falling over the city.

She returned to her apartment and slept through the morning and when she woke, Andrew was waiting for her, sat on a sofa in the living area. He smiled pleasantly, but had the bleary eyes and peaky complexion of someone who also hadn't really slept. "I'm glad you're up," he said. "I wanted to talk to you." He had showered and his damp hair was brushed back and like her he was wearing a dressing gown. "You're not looking too well," he said. "What is it, a headache?"

A headache yes. She nodded.

"Ahh, then I don't really like to bother you with business, except it's a little serious." He picked up a sheaf of bills from the nearby glass table. "These have been accumulating, from your stylist mainly. And I'm really sorry, but I just can't pay at the moment." He watched Renata carefully. She seemed bemused. "As you know," he continued. "I don't make a habit of looking into your expense accounts, but .. I have to say, some items on this bill are a bit surprising .. make up .. one thousand pounds? money lent six thousand.. a loan from your stylist? perfumes ..."

"Give them to me," she said. "I'll pay, don't worry."

"I see. You don't believe me. Let me explain." He stood up and used the remote control to turn on the tv. It was muted but he flicked through the channels, a habit that helped him organise his thoughts. "I invested the moneys I received from your father and our properties and returned you half the interest. I have to say, I saw that interest as your spending money. I never asked you to pay bills, contribute to household expenses."

Renata looked at him. She started to feel guilty.

"As you must understand, it was necessary in these circumstances to make the money yield a high return. It's safe, don't worry! What is left is invested in an excellent affair - split mortgage packages."

"I know that I owe you a lot of money," said Renata. "I don't ask anything from you."

"Oh no please darling. Don't get the wrong idea. It's just St Claire at Vauxhall Credit has been playing some silly games, and Briers and Connolly, those bastards, have been swindling me on materials. That's why I can't pay the bill. You'll forgive me?" He flicked through the channels faster. Renata perceived for the first time that he was nervous. The truth was, he was juggling money so rapidly to cover various borrowings and speculations, there were mornings when he barely had a grand in the bank. St Claire had almost capsized the Credit Agency by embarking on a bulling game against the American investment houses, and only a secret bail out from Eustace to prevent damage to the banking system had saved it. In the meanwhile, Briers and Connolly had outflanked him by buying up land instead of bricks and mortar, leaving them to dictate conditions of sale on the properties they'd been working on together. In need of money, he had loaned his share of the consultancy firm to Larson and was desperate to buy it back, before the lack of stable income was noticed by the banks. And then there was the rent on the Bayswater flat and the money he was sending to Angela, neither of which he dare stop, for fear that Laura would leave him or that Angela would be shrewd enough to instigate legal proceedings before all available cash was swallowed up into a black financial hole. To cover these expenditures, he had been compelled to raise mortgages on theirs and Brandon's apartments.

"I'll pawn some jewellery," said Renata.

"God no," said Andrew, "you can't be seen to do that. If my creditors got wind of it and lost confidence .. no." He stabbed at the buttons on the control.

"Ask my uncle for some money? A loan"

Andrew stopped pressing buttons and turned around. His expression was grateful, forgiving. Of course, this was what he had been aiming for all along. "Really? Do you think you could? Just as a short term measure."

"I'll ask," she said.

His expression turned to one of admiration. "You are a marvellous wife," he said. "If you can get the money into your bank, I'll give you some invoices to sign and it will all be sorted. In fact, it might be a good idea to sign them now, just because I'm going to be so busy." He put down the remote and took some papers from the bottom of the stack of bills, then a pen from a pewter container on the nearby desk. He watched her sign. In truth, her mind was too preoccupied by the previous evening's events for her to give the matter serious attention. She just wanted it out of the way. Andrew beamed happily. "What an excellent wife you are," he said, kissing her on the cheek. "And in the meantime I have another matter to attend to." He went into his own room and proceeded to get dressed. Renata sat down on the sofa and rested her head on her hand. She dozed suddenly and when she came to Andrew had gone and it was getting dark outside the vast panes of glass. The intercom on the door was buzzing. She went over and pressed the button. It was Simone. She let her in, feeling she needed company.

"Andrew not in," Simone asked, looking around the apartment. "I was hoping to discuss..." By her side was the carrier bag stuffed with papers and products that she always carried about with her on business.

Renata shook her head and Simone looked at her, making a rapid evaluation. "It's stifling in here," she said. It was true. The heat was turned up, causing condensation to form against the glass. Renata looked for the remote in order to activate the ventilation. She turned it on and it began to whirr from some unseen location, causing a wave of cool air to filter smoothly across the room. "Are you okay," asked Simone. "You look worried."

"I'm worried, yes," said Renata.

"Money?"

Renata nodded. lowering her eyelids.

"Andrew. He's stopped paying your bills, is that right? And in the meantime, he still has that little apprentice tucked away in Bayswater, paying HER bills."

Renata frowned. She had forgotten to actually consider this. "Yes, that's right," she murmured.

"Tssk," intoned Simone. "And for a woman who looks like you there should be no need to worry. I confess, sometimes I come here to see Andrew, but I'm really here just to get a glimpse of you. You actually are marvellous. Needless to say, if you need money, I can find a dozen men who will give it to you. You can make your choice."

"No, I don't think so. Hochi will take something on account. And I don't want to talk business any more, it's making my head split." She did have an awful headache.

Simone frowned, frustrated. "Well, then there's endorsements of course, look at this." She reached down into her carrier bag and pulled out a jar of white salve. "A new skincare product, vegan or something. I can get you money just for saying on the internet that you use it. It's like I say, a woman like you, there's no reason she can't be independent. And if you ask me, Andrew would be angling for a divorce anyway if you weren't so tied up with your uncle's money. Think about that, then come see me."

Two nights later she was compelled to accompany Andrew and Brandon to a charity ball. Louise and her father were also there, with her and Brandon's engagement soon to be announced, and Andrew hoping that it would bring along some fresh investment from Mr Morrison. Renata told herself that she didn't mind so much, Simone's ideas going some way towards soothing her and allowing her to perceive some new possibilities in her life. They stepped out of their car, her with a large umbrella raised against the showery weather. She entered the ballroom wearing a slightly dampened gold velvet military jacket fringed with pink lace and accented with green plastic buttons over a ruffled peach coloured halter top which exposed her midriff, the ruffles gathered in rows over the top of each other, and then apricot jeans carefully torn at the knees and turned up above the ankles to show off her sandals, delicate creations in gold satin and beaded rose suede. All the men rose to look as she entered. Eustace was present, back from Brussels and he took great pleasure in walking over to congratulate her and allowing them to be photographed together by the press. Afterwards he and Anthony talked for a bit, she heard them mention something about mineral rights. Good lord it never stopped, the endless negotiations.

Later there was an auction and Andrew used some of the money he'd freed up through his arrangement with Mr Cassel to bid on some pearl earrings, a present for Louise. When that bit of business was done, Andrew said that he had to rush off to attend to vital affairs and would be away for three days and would Brandon mind running Rene home later? Louise said she didn't mind, that they could meet the next day, and she would stay to allow people the opportunity to coo over her earrings.

They drove back together in the car. It was really raining now, dense sheets hammering down against the roof, drenching the streets around them and they'd had to dash to the vehicle under cover of her umbrella.

"You still find your fiance amusing then?" asked Renata.

"I do actually," said Brandon, running his fingers through his damp hair so as to dry it. "She was just saying how the artificial canary in Ms Sampson's hat made her look like a cuckoo clock."

"Yes, I noticed that. Didn't sitting there and making bitchy remarks about our contemporaries used to be our hobby?"

"Yes." Brandon smiled wistfully. They arrived back at the development, and he used a control to open the gates and drive into the underground carpark.

"Are you coming up?" asked Renata. "I think there's katsu in the fridge."

"Sure," said Brandon. They got into the apartment and Renata turned round pressing her lips against his and pressing him to the door. It was the people at the ball who'd bored her, the business talk they settled into, the endless quid pro quo. She undid and took off his belt then put it round his neck and looped it so that she had him on a makeshift collar and then tugged it.

"Come along then," she said, "you little bitch" and dragged him towards the bedroom. It was a chamber she had designed and decorated herself, so that layers of crinoline in a rainbow of colours extended out from a clasp above the central light which held a plethora of pastel tinted bulbs in a celtic knot made of wire and filigree. The crinoline reached the walls then dropped down like a tent and here it was separated by billowing masses of stuffed velvet cushions, fashioned into bulbous forms and stitched into the soft suede walls of powder blue so that they poured into the room like clouds of imperial purple, ochre, emerald green .. the carpet was snowy white and in the middle of it all was the bed, the frame in polished bronze and sculpted in the shape of a rose that held its soft round mattress like liquid in a cup. The sheets were quilted in a bewildering patchwork of textiles - Brandon saw daffodils, cartoons, beetles, dots, stripes, hexagons, denim, corduroy, antelopes - and covered with voluminous pillows in downy material and zebra and tiger patterned fur blankets. The furniture surrounding it was made of curved perspex, strawberry pink and apple green, transparent so that you could see the contents of the drawers and wardrobe, with the surfaces of the tables in pink marble and adorned with strange momentos - snowglobes mainly, bejewelled boxes and lamps that resembled strands of alien dna. She opened a drawer and took out a silver case containing cocaine and a narrow tube through which they snorted it and also some pills, which would take an hour or two to kick in. That was okay, they both realised they were in for a long and arduous session.

"Do you remember," he asked afterwards, as they were all curled up in the furs, "when we first met? When you walked into the apartment, dressed like you were, that was when I realised my life had actually changed."

She smiled lazily, abstract, staring at the ceiling. "Yes," she said, "And you had that haircut, but I could tell you were vicious."

"You used to come and pick me up from college, everyone staring at us.. Then we'd go out. You remember .. that time we had to smuggle Madison out of the hotel?"

"That party where they filled the swimming pool with suds and her father had to refurbish the study afterwards. He tried to sue someone didn't he?"

"Yes. Afternoons at Hochi's, I'd watch you all putting together outfits and tell everyone about my time at boarding school."

"You were vicious."

"Well, they didn't used to call it fagging for nothing."

"That you made the new boys dress up as chinese schoolgirls and put on x-rated versions of Gilbert and Sullivan."

He grinned. "Yes, three little maids indeed."

"My god, that explains so much about this country. Later we'd advise each other on our lovers, which ones could be trusted to stay discreet. I suppose that was a kind of proxy for what we really wanted." She looked at him questioningly."

"Yes." He wasn't sure. "Yes, I suppose it was."

He left early the next morning and looked around at the deathly empty spaces, still dripping from the ceased downpour, the dark towering shapes with their sporadically lit condominiums, a chain of broken lights along the river, which smelt faintly of the sea. He congratulated himself silently. He never really believed this was going to happen, but if she was game ... Renata was obviously more aware of his kinks than he was and he had to admit, her being his stepmother gave it that extra kick. And if it all got too weird, he had the marriage to Laura lined up as an exit route. He listened to the wind drive the tidal waters of the river up splashing against the embankment so that they separated out into a spray, then went back to his own apartment.

"You've read this agreement thoroughly?" asked Larson. He was a smallish man with tight wiry hair and a narrow moustache. They were sat in the offices of their consultancy firm, which were surprisingly modest and functional. All the flash was in the meeting room with its long table, slingback chairs and windows that looked out over Wapping. There was a desk, chairs and filing cabinets, a vague effort to suggest a semblance of accountancy.

"Of course I read it, I helped draw it up," said Andrew. "What do you think?"

"It buys back your share of the business unfortunately, but if these payments default, it puts your wife in the hole for twice the amount. Does she realise that?"

"That's my affair."

"It's her uncle I'm thinking of. He gets upset, he might cause a fuss. We don't want anything that brings the regulators sniffing."

"He can't afford a fuss either. It will be fine."

Larson shrugged nonchalantly. "It's your funeral buddy," he said, and cosigned the agreement.

Winter arrived, and with Andrew using it so little, Brandon and Rene moved their affair to the house in Oxfordshire. They spent long coke and ecstacy driven weekends there, screwing in virtually every room and punctuating the downtime with expensive booze and dressing up sessions. Simone had procured her several endorsements that allowed her to continue buying clothes and fund sessions with her stylist, this time for the pair of them, to which Brandon relented, in some ways still treating her like a stepmother. His own fashion ventures had really failed to amount to much and she indulged herself by making him more feminine, applying eyeliner and lipstick, and acted in private as his mistress. Then they spent nights wrapped up in the bearskin rug in front of the fire watching television and sometimes to clear their heads - walks around the grounds near the artificial lake or into the Oxfordshire countryside, everything brittle and frosty. Then coming back, coats covered in ice particles, to disrobe and fuck in the heated conservatory, this time with her electrical taped to one of the tables, coming out naked and laughing with leaves stuck to their skin, no one to see or care. They went to Oxford which inspired her new country style: mohairs and tweeds in shades of raspberry and mustard combined with subdued tartans - violet and mossy green, and then multi pompomed berets. Then Spring came and one day they returned home to find that Andrew was waiting for them. He insisted on talking to Brandon alone. She watched them stroll the neglected, overgrown grounds with a feeling of imminent depression. It was obvious they were discussing the forthcoming marriage to Louise and there were no apparent signs of protest from Brandon. Mr Morrison's money was talking, as her 'uncle's' had done beforehand.

"You see," Andrew was saying as they walked through the grounds. It was fresh, leaves were starting to unfurl on the trees and the long grass was heavy with dew. "I've decided to settle down. That thing with Laura is over, she's moved on. And fair enough, I don't blame her. Probably soon, I'll divorce Renata and try to start things over with your mother. Her architect thing's fizzled out. It will be a bit of fun for the papers, but what's new there? And my brother will be relieved, it was only a matter of time before they found someone in Rene's bed." And without the need to support Renata or keep up the apartment, and the money he sent to Angela covering the divorce settlement anyway, he might save himself from financial disaster, he could have added. He had already persuaded Larson not to bank all of Rene's payments. They could call default and leave the Cassel's with the mess. Get out from under them. Get away from Rene's embarrassments and humiliations with popstars and non-entities. Yes, it was about time.

"And Louise?"

"We'll announce next Wednesday, if that's okay."

Brandon nodded his assent. He had some confused idea that once his father divorced Rene, she might want their affair to be in the open. Christ, what a disaster that would be! And it had run its course. There was something a little unstable about her that would become a burden. He had a feeling about that.

"I want my life to be simpler," said Andrew. "Settle down in the cottage in Suffolk maybe. Not this ridiculous pile. It's time to reduce. You stick with your wife, going forward, that's my advice. Keep life straightforward."

"So, that's it?" said Renata on his return.

"It has to be," said Brandon. "It had to be some time, we both know that."

She looked out through the sitting room window at the garden, dandelions and thistles growing now, among the primulas and geraniums.

"You'll marry yourself one day," he added. "Someone special."

"I have offers."

"That's good."

"No, not really." She started to cry suddenly, shuddering and emitting horrible nasal gasps. Oh goddammit, he thought, how do I get out of here?

"You'll be okay," he said. Then the phone rang in his pocket. It was Patel. Not the conversation he wanted to be having right now, but it had to be better than this. "I have to take this," he said awkwardly. She simply racked her body and made high pitched keening noises, so he went into the hall.

"Patel. What is it?"

There was a hesitation. "Brando .. this is awkward. I don't know how to say this."

"Just say it Patel," he replied with a hint of exasperation.

"You know about that thing with Rene .. how I wanted you to say something. You didn't go through your auntie, did you?"

"Aunt, why? No."

"Its .. she said for money .. Rene might sleep with me, that she had some bad debts coming up. That's not how I wanted it, Brandie. I know you wouldn't do it like that."

Brandon held the phone away from himself, like it was slightly radioactive all of a sudden. "What do you mean debts? What did she say?"

"I don't know, she heard it through Larson."

"Right."

"You didn't do it did you, Brando?"

"No Patel it wasn't me. Listen, you're a good chap."

He walked back into the sitting room. Renata was still sobbing wretchedly, helplessly.

"Rene," he asked, "Did you sign anything?"

She looked up confused, angry actually to be asked suddenly about business. "WHat??!" she spat out, the rasping sound wrenched out of her.

"Did you sign anything, for Andrew?"

"Invoices maybe .. why? What do you care?"

"I think he's been cheating you. Really cheating you."

She looked up uncomprehending through water soaked eyes, some snot coming out of her nose, then her expression cleared slightly. It was feasible. "Stay," she said with an undertone of hope. "Help me .."

When Andrew got out of the elevator and went from the lobby into his apartment he was surprised to see Mr Cassel there along with Renata. Although London had made him very wealthy and he was on the verge of obtaining residency himself, Mr Cassel still retained the style and image of a street trader, with his sheepskin coat and the thick gold chain he wore over his suit, and his scuffed Reebok trainers. He had sprawled himself over one of the leatherbound Eames settees, and was partway through a cigar, the ash of which he was depositing on the oak laminate.

"Ah Andrew," he said. "Those must be the divorce papers, yes."

Andrew was indeed holding the papers. So that was why Cassel was here, but how had he known? He had intended to spring them on Renata before she could lawyer up effectively. "Yes, like we discussed on previous occasions," he said. He looked at the ash.

"We discussed yes," said Cassel, "but I'm afraid to say now there will not be a divorce. Not without a lot of money."

Andrew tried to look stern. "Mr. Cassel, you've done very well out of this. This is not the time for blackmail. You don't want me looking for grounds .. it's expensive for all of us and will end up going against Renata."

"Grounds yes. What about non-consummation of marriage. And I would have understand that actually - if you fuck my niece. She is very nice lady. What I don't understand is, why you fuck WITH my niece." He produced the default statements from a voluminous coat pocket. "Why you fuck with ME, because I lend her the money, yes?!"

Andrew found himself mentally estimating the distance between where he stood and the exit behind him.

"Ah," he said. "Well, that was an agreement she signed of her own accord, to get herself out of a situation of her own making I might add ..."

"And now you are in a situation of your own making." Cassel stubbed the cigar out on the leather of the settee, burning a hole in it. "You need ask yourself, if I steal money in your nice polite English way, back in the former Soviet Union? If sometimes I not have to break a fucking face. Not always myself you understand. Sometimes some man you never see before - who looks like the maintenance man for your .. deluxe condo, that I help you pay for. THAT I HELP YOU FUCKING PAY FOR!!" Cassel jumped to his feet and Andrew squealed, instinctively turning and raising up one leg and shielding his face. After holding this position for thirty seconds he toppled unbalanced to the ground. He had wet himself. Cassel looked down at him for a while then turned towards Renata.

"Divorce maybe not so bad yes. Just get a lot of money." He went out of the apartment, pausing to kick Andrew in the stomach, causing him to emit an audible 'ooof', then got in the elevator.

Brandon came up to the apartment later that evening. He perched awkwardly on the edge of the settee with the burn mark. He noticed it for a second, rubbed it with the edge of his thumb.

"So, you got proper terms from my father?" he asked Renata. She was dressed plainly, in jeans and an old tshirt, and was sat on one of the Starck chairs with two unfinished lines of cocaine on the table next to it and a finished magnum of champagne in the ice bucket to one side.

"Yes," she said. "And soon I'll be divorced, and well off. We can be together."

"We can't. I wouldn't have seen you ruined... you know."

"But you intend to marry still?"

He nodded silently.

"NO!" She stood up, her face distorted.

"Renata! Understand. How can we, with you being who you are. Us being us. For the press to have a field day. People to laugh at us."

"I DOn;t care!! I love you!" She was hysterical.

"We can't!"

"Yes .." She pulled off her t-shirt up over her head to reveal her breasts and pounced over to grab hold of him, ripping at his shirt and trousers. "We can, you'll fuck me." She forced her lips aggressively against his.

"Wh .. renata, stop,"

"No, you'll fuck me." He tried to break free but she pushed him, drove him to the floor, grabbed his flaccid penis. He thought of striking her, making a run for it. Would that end up worse? Jesus, he might as well screw the crazy bitch one more time, then try to escape.

One year later it was summer in Suffolk. Andrew and Brandon were taking a stroll through the village, having left Angela and Louise to play with Claudia, now nearly eight, in the garden.

"So," said Andrew, "your wife's money. What do you plan to do with it? It's wasted just sitting in a bank you know."

"You know some good investments?"

"Maybe. I've been able to do some good work in zoning. Particularly when it comes to redefining the criteria for green belt status. Might even be, there's some land on the edge of this village gets freed up. Imagine what that would be worth!"

"Rather spoil the place though, wouldn't it?"

"Well yes, we'd move. But you would make a killing. Think about it."

"I'll think about it sure."

"Any news of .."

"Rehab again .. the money didn't do her much good."

"Abroad though, safely."

"She saw sense in the end. Especially after Eustace talked to her uncle, and he talked to her family. There's only the mother you know. Her father disappeared after taking part in some sort of protest when she was three, against Chow .."

"Ceaucescu. You could have told me about you and her, really."

"It didn't seem like I could, at the time."

"And you're keeping your nose clean? Got a business in the pipeline?"

"Keeping things out of the papers. I need some profile though, if my brand of skiwear is going to take off."

"Skiing, really?"

"Louise loves it. And it's good fun actually."

They came to a stop outside the old chapel that was now a converted house belonging to a medical contractor. There was a seat outside facing what was once the village green, complete with pond.

"Stay out of split mortgages though," said Andrew as they sat down together, "that's about to fall through. The opportunities there will be in the mess afterwards. Property is going to become a corporate asset."

Brandon looked at the pond. There were no ducks on it. He felt it needed ducks.

3. The belly of the beast

Francis was driving away from the container port when his headlights caught a black huddled mass in the middle of the road. He knew straight away what it was - another one of them. He screeched to a halt, his haulage lorry coming to a stop barely two metres from the prone figure. An illegal it had to be, smuggled in one of the containers and left behind somehow. He got out and went to look at the man. He was dehydrated, barely conscious. Francis poked him with his foot.

"Hey you, can you get up?" he said.

The man groaned, moved slightly. That was something. Francis crouched down, there might be another truck along here soon.

"Hey.. name.." he said. "You have a name?"

The man groaned again. Francis cursed. It meant taking him back to the port authorities. There would be a long wait, a delay. Then he would have to make a statement. Looking round, he started going through the man's pockets until he found a wallet. No money but some ID, fake probably - a slip of paper with an address. He recognised it. It was near Smithfields, accessible.

"Okay pal," he said. "Let's see if we can get you up."

Floret the man's name was. French? Well, some of those African countries had been French. It made sense.

"So, where's this we're going to then?" asked Francis. This Lisa, she a mate of yours?" He chuckled. They were driving along a dark carriageway, lights sporadically streaming across the windscreen. The traffic was medium, they were making headway, the reassuring thrum of moving vehicles around them.

"She is a wife of my brothers." He was drinking from Francis' water bottle.

"Hey, sip that," said Francis, taking one hand off the steering wheel to tilt the bottle away slightly from Floret's lips. "You don't want to get sick."

There was a silence. They passed under a floodlit direction sign.

"So, going to look after you then are they, your brother?"

"Yes."

"Is HE legal?"

"Yes, he was able to come. Myself I had problems because of the politics."

"Yeah, you want to stay well clear of that." They were reaching the edge of the city now, and traffic would slow them down no matter what the time of evening.

"Look behind the seats," said Francis. "There should be a spare jacket and a hat."

"I am not cold."

"It's not for the cold you ninny. So you look like you belong in the truck. Like a spare driver you understand? Anyone twigs you, I'll be in dead lumber."

Floret understood very well, the first part anyway. He fumbled around behind the seats until he found the required clothing and put it on. Francis looked over approving.

"There you go," he said. "Just a regular Tom, Dick and Harry."

He dropped Floret two streets over from the address.

"Next left, two streets over, have you got that?" He was sat in the cab, looking down at the man, who had seemed mesmerised by the scale of the city as they passed through. Exhaust from the engine blew back down the street in between them. Floret nodded.

He revved up the truck again and wondered whether to say good luck. He guessed that was the formality, but not wanting to bear responsibility for the man's fate, he simply said, "See you later, eh," and drove off. That was his good deed done. Maybe Amnesty International would give him an award, he thought, chuckling as he circled to get back on the highway.

'Lisa's' was a cafe near to the Smithfield market. Floret could see that it was closed but tried the door anyway. He looked up, there were flats or something like them above the cafe. Did his brother live there? He wandered about a bit until it got light. The market must have been busy but now it was winding down. People were driving away and the lights flickered out one by one and then the shutters rolled up, making a tremendous rattle - clack, clack, clack, clack. He went for a closer look but a security guard noticed and stepped in his direction, a black shadow against the bright light behind him.

"Can I help you?" the man asked. The uniform alone brought unpleasant connotations. Floret shuddered and walked back into the streets.

His brother Kenge did in fact live above the shop, so that when he came down that morning, the dim dawn just leaking in, and rolled up the blinds he found what he first thought was his own reflection staring back at him, in the glass pane of the door. But as he was a portly man, this reflection morphed down and slimmed until he realised he was looking at his brother, but so haggard and drawn and made faint by the glass, he thought he was staring at a ghost. In fact, for a full minute he was convinced that his brother was dead and he was seeing his spirit. Then Floret smiled and moved up to the pane and mouthed 'brother', and the truth hit him like a blow. He unbolted the door rapidly and drew him inside.

"Floret, my god, my god, what happened?"

" .. long story .." said Floret. Then collapsed weakly onto the tiles of the cafe floor.

"LISA!!" shouted Kenge. "LISA."

The blonde woman appeared, dressed but no make up, hair uncombed and tangled. At first, she thought it was some homeless man who'd been sheltering in the doorway, but Kenge's expression made that assumption wrong somehow.

"Floret," he said. "It's Floret." She rushed over to look at him. "We need to get him upstairs," she said. "Into a bed."

When Floret came round, forty eight hours later, he was in a spare room above the shop on a mattress, wrapped in some mixed combination of blankets. Kenge was watching him. There was a bowl of water by the makeshift bed, a sponge, paracetamol. Kenge smiled widely.

"I hadn't got a call or message from you in a year. I thought you were dead. I honestly thought you were dead." A tear filled his eye and spilled down over his cheek.

"... no..." the man shook his head.

"But hungry, my god you must be hungry."

"I am."

Kenge turned to where a young girl was peering through the doorway. "Go to your mother," he said. "Tell her to bring up some food, something plain." Once he had heard her trot down the stairs, he looked down more seriously.

"So, what happened, how did you get here?"

"I paid some men. I'd buried some money before they arrested me."

"Arrested. Ah brother, you made too many enemies with your preaching. Is it bad there now?"

"The government are back in control. They drove the militias out of Timbuktu and across the border. The men, they gave me a new name."

"Yes, we found it. Dmabi - will it hold up?"

"They said so."

"Yes well. We need to find out for sure."

Lisa came in carrying soup. "How is he?" she asked.

"Weak. Can he stay here?"

"He's your brother," she said. "Of course, he stays here."

Lisa had met Kenge when he was working as a delivery driver, dropping off produce from a depot in Leicester to the grocery stall she was working on at the market back home. She was miserable at the time, trying to hide her wages from her father, hoping to get away, her sister pregnant and Anthony furious, taking it out on the rest of them. Kenge had a relation in London he said. He was good company also, laid back in a way that she envied. They went there and worked at his uncle's import business, sorting out the produce, the stacked crates of papaya, yams and okra, saving what they could and when the cafe became available, they had borrowed extra money and bought it. Kenge was worried at first, but Lisa said, it being so close to the market it would be a difficult business to make fail, and she was right of course. They moved into the flat above the cafe and got married at last. She told no one from her own family, the only people who came were the friends they'd made in London.

It took several months for them to sort out Floret's documentation, and of course it was necessary for Kenge to pass him off as a cousin and get used to calling him by his new name. The bulk of the arrangements had been made by a poultry dealer by the name of Bahrim, who frequently employed illegals, taking their free labour as payment for his services in arranging, sometimes fraudulently, their right to remain. It should be mentioned that this debt of labour did not cease once the documentation had been organised, and that most times a significant 'overdraft' had accrued, to be paid out of the client's legal wages when the time came. So, for these months Floret found himself gutting poultry, in a blue plastic cap, apron and gloves, cutting out the organs and separating them from the viscera which were dumped in a polyethylene tub, then moving crates of chicken skins, the tepid fluid leaking from the sides, or separated meat parts into the freezer, as though London didn't seem cold enough to him already, horribly oppressive, damp and grey.

The rest of the time, once he had washed to get the scent of dank meat out of his skin, he loafed around the cafe. It was neat and trim, with a steady influx of people: drivers, porters, part time workers. On one wall, facing the front entrance was a painting of glistening offal, obviously done from one of the market stalls.

"Who did that?" he asked Lisa. She answered, although somehow 'Dmabis' presence around the cafe had started to irritate her. The fact was he wasn't easy company. There was something in his bearing that spoke of a silent grudge, a hurt pride. Well, he had been a teacher back in his own country and now he was stacking meat. It was more than that though. It was like he'd always had it and he wordlessly criticised you for not being able to meet the values he'd established within himself.

"My nephew," she said. "He comes down to the market to make sketches. I'll introduce you."

Dmabi looked at the painting again. The colours weren't right, in his opinion.

"I've had it with painting anyway," said Aaron. He was sat with Dmabi on some chairs outside the cafe, facing the rear of the marketplace with its facade of red brick and Portland stone. Not too far down was the carved gable above its rear exit, rampant dragons at each corner. They had been introduced to each other by Lisa, and found themselves, somehow, in the habit of sitting outside and chatting now and again. "Spent weeks on it. Weeks. And what is it? A failure. I can't stand it." He was in a terrible mood.

"What about the one at Lisa's?" said Dmabi.

"What?"

"The one in the cafe."

"Stupid really. I should have put a foot through it and now I can't. I'm stuck with it."

"The colours were wrong."

"Well .. they were allegorical. I was trying to get over something about the mechanics of life, you know?"

"But the colours were wrong."

Aaron looked over at the older man. He could see that he was completely intractable. It was interesting, in its way.

"Well yeah," he said, "there was that as well." They sat for a while longer and he felt the irritation build up again.

"What do you make of that Dmabi?" he nodded towards a stretch of wall that had been garlanded with posters, some proclaiming 'leave' and some 'remain'. "Well, since you've no reason to give a damn, I'll tell you what I think - it's not going to make a bit of difference either goddamn way. There might as well be two signs saying up and down, or dog and cat. Complete fucking sham, a class war in disguise. Which status quo do we settle for? The only revelation was: how stupid they still think working people are. 'You voted the wrong way, you have to do it again' - like errant school children being told off by the swots. The psychic shock that not everyone assumed they were right about everything. Of course, they really went back to feeling contempt for us the time they realised we'd lost interest in holding their revolution for them, the one that would have seen the chattering classes step up one place and run things, like they feel they ought to be doing. So now they've stopped patronising us and they despise us again and it's fair enough. But mark it, they'll be patronising your mob next, hoping you'll rise up. You want my advice, don't fall for it. Don't fucking fall for it."

Then Aaron thrust himself off the bench, picked up his duffel bag and strode furiously down the street. Dmabi watched him. The British obviously had their own cultural faultlines, but beyond that, he found the young man's concerns fairly nonsensical.

After hours in the cafe, they were preparing food for the next day. Kenge's real ambition was to have a restaurant, so although the cafe had started off selling traditional worker's fare - bacon, sausage and eggs - he had gradually tweaked the menu to incorporate some 'proper' meals - stews and gumbos. But even for the breakfasts they tried to get the best cuts and produce from the market. That evening they were discussing haggis with Angus from the slaughterhouse.

"It's a good use of offal" he was saying. "A hunter's dish basically. Take out the animal's stomach, clean it out and stuff it with chopped up heart, lungs, liver like a carrybag. I add suet, barley, herbs."

"It's good to use all of the animal." said Kenge. He was busy putting pork through a grinder, much to Dmabi's disgust.

"Agreed," said Angus. "Even the blood and intestines, let it coagulate for black pudding. Marrow from the bones for suet. Jellied hooves. Only thing I won't eat is the brains. That's too much like eating the animal's thoughts, although I've heard of it being done."

The girl Pauline, who was by the back door, playing with the stray cat they called 'Mutton', turned round and said, "Dmabi, tell the story of the men who got eaten."

"Eaten?" he murmured, coming out from some internal thoughts of his own.

"She must have heard you talking to Bahrim," said Lisa.

"Tell it again, please," begged Pauline. Dmabi looked over at Lisa, who nodded her assent. Pauline put down the cat, scampered over and jumped up onto Dmabi's knee.

"Well," he said. "It starts with a man who was put in prison."

"Why," asked Pauline.

"He had his belief, and other people wanted him to say he was wrong."

"And if he had, his life might have turned out better," said Kenge, who was chopping onions now.

Dmabi ignored him. "This prison was far away from anywhere, in a place that was hot and the conditions unsanitary, and sometimes the prisoners who were slow to follow orders got beaten by the guards. Sometimes they got beaten by the guards anyway. Some got sick and unable to work and the guards did not care to look after them so for their own amusement they took them down to the river and threw them to some crocodiles. You could hear them screaming even though the prison was a mile away."

"That's terrible," said Lisa, slightly shaken.

"There's no fun to that," said Angus. "That's why I value my own profession. There's mercy to be found at the end of a butcher's knife, better for a cow than being eaten alive by lions anyway."

"But that's not the man who got eaten," said Pauline.

"No," said Dmabi. "There was this one time when they wanted to show the prisoners how impossible it was to escape. There was a man who had tried a few days before. He had got quite far but then grew fatigued and tried to rest underneath an acacia tree. Once he rested he was too weak to move again. An army of ants found him and started to feast. He was too weak to crawl very far. They ate him alive bit by bit and it must have taken quite a long time. When we got there, there were still ants on the body picking clean the husk. Its the one crawling out of the eye sockets I remember. The eyes and gums and .. other parts .. are soft and go first, then they go through the orifices and eat out from the inside. I think a man might go mad actually, before he died."

There was quiet for a bit. "Did the prisoners stay there?" asked Lisa.

"No. There was some fighting not far away and all the guards just took up their weapons and left. The prisoners even found a bus in a compound with enough fuel to take them to a town. The only problem was they were weak and hungry with no money and had to steal food on the way, and then of course when they got home, their names were still on a list. So, one of them: he found some money he had buried and escaped here."

Kenge by this time was busy tasting the stock. "Mmmmm", he said. There was a knock in the door.

"Who on earth is that?" said Lisa, glad to be distracted and went out of the kitchen into the cafe. She came back with Bahrim.

"It's good news," she said.

"I've found you a proper job," Bahrim said to Dmabi, "porter at Billingsgate market. At the agreed arrangement of course." The arrangement was twenty percent kickback to Bahrim and the supervisor.

"Isn't that great?" said Lisa. Kenge looked over and nodded. It was fine by him.

"I mean, it's a start," she said, "Then maybe you could find a job as a tutor or something."

Dmabi looked around. Mainly what he wanted was to get away from this filthy place where people handled pigs and pig's blood. Get away from all this food. There was too much, it made him feel sick. "Okay," he said. "Yes."

Lisa was delighted. "It's a good start," she said. "It will get you on your feet."

"What are you thinking?" she asked Kenge later, as they lay together in bed.

"Just of my brother's story. It was the first time I heard it. I never knew he had suffered so much."

"To be imprisoned like that, just because of your beliefs, its barbaric."

"Yes. But you did not ask what those beliefs were."

"No. Why, what were they?"

"That women should always be covered. That the traditional tribal dancings be forbidden. That people who commit adultery should be stoned to death."

"Ah. But now he's here, maybe he'll change. Learn to be more moderate."

"You have to understand .. when our parents were gone, he brought me up. He used to work in that school, and the children were terrible. You could not get all of them to sit still and behave for more than five minutes and he would finish work exhausted and infuriated. Then he would walk back four miles and on the way do the shopping and come back and cook me tea. Then he would see me eat and he would smile, and all I'd been doing all day, was playing by the river with my friends. But he would smile, because he had done his job."

Lisa cuddled up against Kenge's big belly. "He'll be okay" she said. "Once he starts work."

The supervisor at Billingsgate was a pale scraggy man called Quayle who was swathed against the cold in a variety of fleeces, gloves and jerkins, over which he'd draped his hi viz jacket. The porters as an established institution had now been replaced with casual labour doing irregular hours, just as the market itself had been moved from the City to the Isle of Dogs, near to the fancy waterfront developments at Canary Wharf. Most of the porterage started when the container lorries began rolling in during the afternoon. Dmabi watched as the consignments came in, unloading from their refrigerated wagons amidst the breathless vapours of evaporating cold: cod, keeling, whiting, flounders, plaice, dabs, eels, skate, turbot, brill, bass, herring, mullet. Then the shrimps and oysters and mussels, dashes of pink and black among the iridescent silvers and oily greys. There was the strong perpetual odour of fish. By midnight the wholesalers were arranging their produce and the auctions started around two thirty in the morning and the mongers and restaurateurs would start to arrive and the place became a massive hubbub of shouting and bartering. Dmabi found that he lacked the easy manner of the rest of the marketplace and did not always understand its ribald sense of humour, and so most people there got into a habit of omitting him from the conversation, even when he was standing close by. He also began to feel he was getting in the way of Lisa and Kenge's marriage by hanging around the spare room or the cafe, but fortunately Bahrim was able to help him integrate further, by introducing him to the members of a social club who met not too far away in Bow. This innocuous society, which held its meetings in a utility building at the base of a block of high rise flats, got together on irregular occasions to discuss matters of concern: business dealings, family worries and political problems too: the lack of religious teaching in mainstream education, the deplorable dress, attitude and behaviour of women in the country, and the pervasive, evil, permissiveness all around them, which they felt was being encouraged by certain ethnic groups. The contacts made by Dmabi via this new cohort helped him find the tutoring jobs he'd been hoping for, part time cash in hand work helping children from migrant families understand the work they brought back from school, sometimes even going so far as to 'correct' what they were being taught.

One night Lisa was cleaning the cafe and she watched Dmabi come downstairs, nod his head goodbye and set off towards one of his tutoring jobs. He left behind him the faint odour of fish. She watched his silhouette blend with the gathering shadows of the rest of the night, then put down her scouring pads and went upstairs herself to the small room that she occupied with her husband. He was sat on the bed in his nightgown, browsing some recipes on the internet and making notes, planning for the day when they might have a restaurant serving Mali cuisine.

"Your brother's been working for a while now, it's strange he doesn't seem to be searching for a flat," she said.

Kenge looked up from his tablet so that the blue light shone on his face and smiled apologetically. "It is London," he said. "And lots of the money he makes he has to use to pay his debt."

"And what about his tutoring work?"

"I am sorry," said Kenge. "Is my brother burdensome to you?"

"Only that the parent of one of his pupils came into the cafe today. She had found this in his exercise book." Lisa handed over a creased notepad sized piece of paper. On one side had been written some multiplication tables. The other side was glossily printed and in bold fiery letters read: 'the Bonfire of the West." Below it, on a stark black background, angry red letters laid out the rationale for an inevitable forthcoming holy war. "This is what he is teaching," she said. "We cannot have it here. It's going to ruin everything."

Kenge took hold of the piece of paper and read it and groaned, looking tired. "He never learns," he said, leaning back against the wall. "He never changes."

"I thought being here and having a job, he'd see the opportunities. But this is just a spit in the face. You think we're going to have a restaurant once Facefrend knows we've been sheltering a jihadi? We won't even have a cafe. It's a spit in the damn face."

Kenge closed his eyes and screwed up his face. From his head somewhere he heard the sound of laughter, him and his friends playing by the river.

Quayle was in his office when Dmabi came in looking tired and limping. He'd been lifting and transporting heavy crates with the sack cart, moving them out of the frozen trailers onto the sudden warmth of the quay and then into the market through the crowds of porters and traders. Feeling had just come back into his fingers and his muscles were aching and one of the other porters, who had taken a dislike to him had 'accidently' dropped some skate in front of him so that he'd slipped, the heavy sack cart of turbot banging against his calf as he fell. There had been laughter and then the man had come over all mock concern.

"Sorry about that Idi mate, are you alright?" Among themselves they had given him the nickname Idi Amin, even the carribeans and women and polacks.

"Heard you had an accident," said Quayle from behind his desk. It had clipboards holding sheafs of paper, a computer and then odd items such as screwdrivers and paperclips scattered across it, surrounding a thermos flask.

"I slipped yes."

"Hurt your leg. You can still work?"

"I will work."

"Got something for me?"

Dmabi took a fold of ten pound notes out of his trouser pocket and passed it over.

"Very good," said Quayle, putting the money in the top desk of the drawer. He looked at Dmabi for a minute.

"You need to come down off your high horse for a bit Idi, make an effort to get along."

"I don't like that they call me Idi."

"Its banter thats all. Like how we call the other African lad Bongo, or the Polish Boris and Ivan."

"But how is it funny all the time? Like the same joke they make about their wives smelling like the fish." He curled up his lip in distaste.

"You need a sense of humour, that's all."

"Or like how they call you the stupid Angle."

"I'm sorry?"

"Stupid Angle. It's banter."

"Right ... okay, I see." Quayle didn't look impressed. He let Dmabi stand there a while. "Well, I can't afford to have the Safety Commission knocking around. I don't need to do you any favours either. One more accident and you're out on your ear, understand?"

"Yes."

"Good." He watched Dmabi leave. Smartarse bastard, he thought. Lets see how he gets on with a few less shifts.

Out in the summer warmth the aroma from the fish market had become swollen and more pervasive and seemed to have permeated Dmabi's skin. Kenge could sense it wafting towards him as they stood across from the corrugated metal hall, the tarmac outside being hosed down, washing the decaying morsels spilled overnight into the Thames. His attitude towards the older, leaner man was apologetic, almost cringing.

"You can see that there's going to be trouble if you stay. Lisa is upset about it."

"You should learn to control your wife. It's disgraceful how she goes about uncovered, swapping dirty jokes with the men in the cafe. Don't you see what will happen? And your daughter will turn out the same."

Kenge's attitude changed. "But you never married, did you brother?" he said. "I wonder why .. I know I can't repay my debt, but I've tried to show you the city. You won't come for drinks with my friends. Okay, you have friends of your own ..

but they all think the same .. they are bringing you the same trouble you ran into back home. Don't you see that?"

"And don't you see what is happening to you? All that disgusting pork you handle, it has made your body corpulent. I don't want to think what it is doing to your soul. I will just be glad to get away from it. Relieved. The pair of you are like pigs in a sty, surrounded by decadent filth. You're the one who doesn't see, but that is my fault - I raised you to be too happy. Now your sins are on my shoulders."

Kenge was tense, staring back through slitted eyes. "I don't want to see you at the cafe again. Not until you have apologised for what you just said."

"No. You will come to me, if God lifts the scales from your eyes. One day you will see yourself in the dirt and remember what I have said, then you will understand that I spoke to you as a brother."

"You have somewhere to go?"

"My friends will find me a flat."

"Please .. be careful." Kenge tried to lay a hand on his brother's arm but Dmabi shrugged it off.

"Don't worry about me," he said. "Worry about yourself." Then he limped away from the dock in the direction of the tube station.

Pauline and her friend Michael were in a playground near the infant's school they both attended. Michael's mother Sandra worked in a cheese shop across from the market and so was acquainted with Lisa, and on odd days collected Pauline from school and dropped her off at the cafe. She was letting them run around and play on the swings and roundabout a while as she enjoyed a cigarette and gossiped with one of the other mothers, Lauren.

"That cousin of theirs has moved out now, hasn't he?" said Lauren. "You have to admit, that was an odd arrangement."

"They were waiting for his paperwork to come through," Sandra replied. "It takes ages apparently. That's if he was legal."

"You think he wasn't?"

"Just that he was working with Bahrim. There's a lot of whispers about him, the people he takes on at the processing plant."

"You wouldn't say anything though."

"No, of course not. Her and Kenge are institutions now."

Still, the pleasant tingle of gossip was lingering as she went over to drag Michael and Pauline away protesting from the roundabout. Soon enough she had them put together with their coats and bags and they were all on their way.

"I heard your cousin Dmabi's moved out now Pauline," she said. "There must be more room at the flat."

"Yes," said Pauline, "and it doesn't smell of fish!"

"Aww, you must miss him though."

"Yes, he told me about a crocodile."

"A crocodile, gosh! Was that in Africa?"

"Yes. Some man escaped from prison! And then he was eatens by antses."

"Mum! Mum!" interjected Michael. "He had to leave because of the jihadi. Pauline said."

"That was a secret!" squealed Pauline.

Sandra stopped in her tracks. She crouched down swiftly and looked the children square in the face.

"What jihadi?" she asked sternly. "Tell me."

Pauline looked upset. "It was an argument between mummy and daddy," she said. "I wasn't meant to listen."

"That's okay, I'm mummys friend," said Sandra. "But you need to tell me, so mummy doesn't get in trouble. It's very important."

Pauline shook her head stubbornly. Sandra turned to Michael. "Michael?"

"We don't know mum. Just that they were angry at Dmabi and Bahrim because of a jihadi. And they don't call him Dmabi when they argue, they call him Floret."

"Right, okay." Sandra stood up flustered. This was a damn pickle, no doubt. Enough to go on one of her cheeses.

"Are you sure about this?" said Bahrim. Aaron nodded sternly. He had found Dmabi at the fish market, ostensibly there to do some sketches, but really to ask the favour, and that was for Bahrim to show him round one of the slaughterhouses. He was still interested in mechanics. The mechanics of the universe he had explained as they walked out of the white tiled tube station nearby.

"Although there are times, I would rather have been something straightforward, like a proper mechanic. I mean you fix a car, and you know it's fixed, and you know why you fixed it. Painting is like trying to fix a camel with a spanner you know."

"So why do it?" asked Dmabi.

"Trying to release something inside. It's lodged in there, but I won't know what it is until I scoop the damn thing out."

"It's dissatisfaction. The universe isn't good enough for you. You think you can beat it but you can't."

"And what about you, the reason why you left my aunt's. I mean I haven't been told clearly but I can guess. You didn't like it?"

"My brother lives uncleanly."

And now they were in the yard of the processing plant. The packed cages of poultry had been unloaded and one by one were placed at the head of the conveyor belt. The operator cranked open the cage, and its chickens tumbled down a steel ramp onto the moving belt where they clucked and tried to take their bearings. They were overfed shortly before arrival to make them more docile, Bahrim explained. The conveyor belt moved them inside and plastic enshrouded workers picked them up and hung them upside down, squawking and flapping, by their feet onto steel clamps on an overhead rail that took them inevitably towards the slaughterman who slit through the carotid artery and surrounding nerves with his knife, all in one go, letting the blood spurt down into the sluice, which emptied it into the vats where it would coagulate and become fertiliser. Aaron watched the methodical messy harvest. "He does that all day. Minute after minute for hours?" he asked.

"Hundreds of chickens to get through," said Bahrim.

Once they were bled out, the machinery dunked the birds into boiled water that loosened the feathers so that they were swiftly plucked, virtually falling out to render them bald, then they were moved onto a new belt that passed between two bandsaws that hacked off the feet and heads and these were gathered up and thrown into waste barrels. Aaron realised this was the picture he wanted - a barrel of severed chicken heads staring up at you, then another all of feet, sad, helpless. He went over to take photographs with his phone.

"This is the one. This is enough." he said.

"What is it you think you are looking at here," asked Dmabi. "The workings of society or the universe?"

"I haven't decided yet. Maybe the universe without grace."

"You don't want to see the evisceration?" asked Bahrim

"What does that involve?"

"Removal of the heart, liver and kidneys. Packaging into separate baggies. Vacuuming out of the lungs. Arrangement of the entrails for inspection."

"No, there's no need." He took eighty pounds from his pocket, and as arranged gave it to Bahrim. As this was happening there was a commotion out in the yard. A battered Vauxhall had swung into the compound and a young man leapt out of the driver's seat and ran into the shed.

"It's immigration," he gasped. "They're coming here."

Bahrim cursed and ran over to the control panel, pushing the large buttons that sent the surrounding carousel of slaughter grinding to a halt.

"Immigration!!" he shouted "Overalls off. Out Out!!"

The young man ran to open a steel door that allowed exit from the plant straight into the back street. He started to motion the workers, dragging the more confused and reluctant ones out himself. "Out, fucking out!!" Where necessary resorting to kicks or slaps.

"You too." Bahrim said to Dmabi, "out the front with your friend but slow, casual. Wait for us at the carwash." Dmabi nodded and they strode out, Aaron going along compliantly. He hadn't expected the extra excitement. Halfway down the street they saw the white vans scream past - Immigration Control inscribed on the side.

They were waiting outside the unused carwash around twenty minutes, sat on its low whitewashed kerb. Then the

Vauxhall came around the corner and pulled up adjacent to them. The young man got out.

"They want to see Bahrim's paperwork, all registered workers, permits. Probably they'll take him in."

"It's just immigration?" asked Dmabi.

"For now. But they've been to your flat in Bow too. That's what gave me the heads up. I went to pick up the discs. They had them and all the literature too. I figured if they had the flat they were on to your workplace, so I drove up to the overpass to see if there were any other vans coming this way .." He paused for breath.

"The flat is no good?"

"Its fucked. Who do you think did it .. your brother?"

"He might have, I don't know."

"Who else?"

Dmabi stayed silent.

"Well, its fucked. Where else can you go?"

Dmabi thought a while then looked at Aaron.

"Sure, sure," said Aaron. "For a few days."

Aaron lived in a cramped apartment above a takeaway in Whitechapel. It was getting dark when they arrived, a bunch of youths spilling out of the takeaway grasping cans of soft drink and cartons of fried chicken and fries. Aaron looked at the crispy coated legs, the end product, until it went through the body's own processing facilities anyway. He unlocked a door to the side of and separate from the takeaways entrance and led Dmabi up some stairs, onto a landing, then into his rooms.

"Heat comes up from downstairs," he said. "So most of the time you don't need the radiators on. Sweltering in the summer though." There was a living space and kitchen in one room, and half of that served as a studio. A sofa and table were pushed up against one wall, to the side of the window, and in the centre of the room was an easel and a cheaply veneered table holding jars of mixed colours or white spirit, old margarine tubs now holding tubes of paint or splayed brushes, rags. Canvases were stacked against the wall facing the sofa and a few had been hung for the purposes of display. Two of these were nudes and Dmabi's lip curled up in distaste.

"I'll make some tea," said Aaron. "Hungry?"

"A little." Aaron went 'into' the kitchen and sorted out some cleanish mugs and plates. "Mm, not much in," he said. "You like peanut butter?"

"Peanut butter is good." Dmabi was trying to make space for himself on the sofa, which involved moving aside carrier bags filled with magazines.

"Yeah, sorry for being so English. I collect clippings you know, I'd have to find it, but there was one story: a family came back from holiday in France. Went inside then back out to fetch the luggage, found this guy wandering about outside.

They figured out he'd been hanging onto the underneath of their mobile home, for three days! trying to get into the country. The bit of the story that stuck in my head - 'realising the man must be hungry' - after hanging onto the underneath of a car for three days you mind - 'they offered him a packet of Mini Cheddars." Aaron laughed uproariously. "Didn't go inside and cook him a meal you notice, fucking packet of mini cheddars, after three days!!! That is too fucking English. I have the photo somewhere. The whole family was plump. Need I say more." He brought over the sandwiches and cups of tea.

"These are fine," said Dmabi.

"Yeah well, you don't look as though you eat much, as a rule."

"You paint food," said Dmabi. He nodded across to one of the paintings on the wall, which was of some squashes in orange and green.

"Did that one in Covent Garden. The mechanics of life. Ripe, bursting to achieve their potential. They do that then they wither. And that's okay. The crime is when you wither having never ripened."

"Every seed knows what it is meant to be." said Dmabi. "But it need to be planted in the proper soil. The ground needs to be prepared."

"Exactly. The ground here is fallow."

"No, it is poisoned. You think you can match creation. This is your arrogance."

"Me. Personally?"

"Yes. Only God can make things in an image. When you attempt to copy you mock him and create cheap travesties."

"Then why did he make us creative. Why give us that impulse?"

"It is a temptation, like the others."

"But those temptations have an approved outlet, marriage for example."

"The outlet for the spirit is in the glorification of god."

"For the communal spirit. What about the individual, to express himself?"

"Express yourself!" Dmabi snorted. "What do you think is going on inside you that is so important, so unique, compared to the entirety of creation? It is an arrogance, an attempt to raise yourself up."

"Strange that, Dmabi. I would have said pride was one of your defining qualities."

"You spent hundreds of years trying to copy reality, but how can you achieve it? Now you are drowning in images. The copy has become more important to you than the original. In the end you gave up, and now try to express yourself, thinking every little impulse or notion you have is interesting to the universe. It is of no interest, except to a child. That is how children think."

"But people do think in different ways. That's the problem. I have no doubt you're a brave man. There's the one thing that terrifies you: that someone thinking or living in a different way renders your own existence 'wrong' somehow, that your life is a waste. But that's what scares everyone. It's the system we find to cope that matters. It's what makes the systems."

"No. There is a right way and a wrong way. Even your scientists, they are looking for One Answer to everything yes? The one that satisfies all their equations. So, there is a truth, a single perspective."

"Right or wrong. Up or down. Cat or dog. What if the perspective changes, infinitely, all the time? What if there are an infinite number of ways, of truths and perspectives?"

"Then God is the only one who can see them, and the words he has given us are the ones that allow us to function in such a universe. They teach us our place."

"Words written in stone. You know somebody, tired of all the discussion, wrote those down one day and said 'look, I've written that down, now they can't be changed, you have to agree with me and I will always be right. I don't have to doubt'. Words are a psychological trap. That's why you're better relying on your conscience."

"And the words come from our conscience, which was put there by God."

"Yeah, well .... yeah."

Dmabi frowned then, but didn't say anything. The takeaway sign had started to flash against the window, red then white, red then white, a hazy glow. Aaron left him curled up in spare blankets on the sofa. The next morning when he woke up and went into the front room, Dmabi had gone, leaving the blankets scrunched up to one side. He had also taken down the two nude portraits and slashed them with a kitchen knife. They had been two of his best works.

"The son of a bitch," thought Aaron. "Only I get to do that."

Lisa went across the road to the cheese shop that Sandra worked in. It had a fine selection, the best of continental as well as produce from across the country. She liked the cheeses in big wheels behind the counter, they looked so dewy and wholesome, whites, yellows and oranges. She licked her lips. "Two slices of Mont D'Ors and a Cantal," she said.

"So, the restaurant, it's going ahead?" asked Sandra, as she cut out the slices.

"Once we've sold the cafe and rented out the flat, yes. I'm afraid it will end up being something more fancy, a brasserie or what have you."

"Well, your restaurant will be fancy too won't it, over in the West End."

"We hope so, there's quite a buzz about it anyway, social media wise."

"And what about your cousin, did you ever hear from him?"

"Since Bahrim got charged, no." She lowered her voice. "Do you think people think ill about us, that we put him up, helped him get papers?"

"Some. But most people know you look out for family no matter what, that's how it works around here."

"They questioned us for ages, nearly charged us. But I think they were hoping, if they didn't, he might be lured back."

"They don't know where he is?" Sandra paused in wrapping up the cheese to look seriously at Lisa, who glanced back. Both women found themselves wondering about the other, what exactly they knew.

"No, he just disappeared."

She walked out of the shop and looked round at all the faces. A small sample among the thousands, millions of people that surrounded her. Who knew what they were all thinking? She tucked the cheeses under her stout arm. It felt reassuring.

The restaurant was exuberantly styled, with deep red walls, the decor some way between West African and English. It was called Kenge's. Lisa had considered trying to get Renata Cassel, who'd been married once to her rich cousin, for the interior but contact between the two halves of the family had long been lost. The designer they hired went for that sort of vibe anyway and most people agreed that he'd succeeded. The food was getting good reviews, but there was always the danger that was the novelty factor. Kenge though was happy and soon was learning to run the kitchen like a professional, with Lisa being front of house. They were a formidable team. One night the waiters, and the cooks and maitre'd had gone home, and they were outside closing up the restaurant when Lisa saw Floret across the street staring at them. He was dressed in dark clothes, a wool cap pulled low over his head.

Lisa's heart palpitated and she unfroze herself just enough to be able to tap Kenge on the shoulder as he stooped to lock the shutter. He turned his head, then after a moment saw his brother too. He stood up.

"Floret," he started, "where did you ... it wasn't us, you know that? I promise."

"I know," said Floret.

"Are you safe, are they after you?"

"I'm on a list, but they don't look hard."

"You should come one night, eat. Something just for you. It will be good."

Floret laughed. "No, I just wanted to see, that's all. You are happy brother?"

"I am, and you, are you .. "

"It makes me feel better somehow .. it shouldn't"

"Brother , co ..."

"Goodbye," Floret said curtly, then turned and walked away into the darkness. They didn't hear about him again until the incident in Liverpool.

4. The pen is mightier than the sword

"Mum, I've torn my skirt look", said Deliah, sliding open the patio doors. She was a tall girl of fourteen.

"Let me have a look," said Martha. It was a mild September afternoon, around six o' clock and she was sat out on a terrace looking out over the garden. Deliah came over and passed her the skirt. "It's not too bad, I can embroider it," said Martha. "Go get my kit." Deliah did as she was told and then they spent the next ten minutes in silence as Martha invisibly sewed up the tear. It was quiet and peaceful in the garden, just the breeze in the trees in the fields behind the converted farmhouse and the twitter of sparrows. Then the two boys came strolling down the lane from the bus stop up at the junction, late from college.

"Hi mum," said Oliver. "Sorry we're late, there was something happening in town." He seemed a little tipsy.

"Something happening in a pub," Martha observed.

"Well, yes."

"Never mind," sighed Martha, "the lasagne just needs heating up."

"Oh great, thanks mum."

"Simon," said Deliah, disconcerted, remembering her dilemma from two hours earlier. "We lost one of the chickens, the silver one."

Simon, the slightly younger one, laughed. "What do you mean we lost it?"

"It's gone, come look." She ran over to the coops against the high stone wall to the left.

Oliver scoffed. "You were playing with them this morning, letting them run around. I bet you forgot to lock the cage."

But Delilah hadn't heard, she was peering in through the wire with Simon.

"I'll have to go look around see if I can find it," he murmured, unconvinced of the potential success of the operation.

Oliver laughed. "All you're going to find is feathers, if that. Some cat or fox will have got it by now. That's what you get for being free range I guess." He laughed again.

"Oliver!" Martha scolded.

"Oh, you are a beast," said Delilah. She was weepy.

"What was happening in town?" asked Martha, to change the subject.

"Girls," said Oliver, and Martha sadly rolled her eyes. Simon had pulled a book out from his knapsack, pushed up his glasses and followed Oliver inside. "Save some lasagne for your father," Martha called. Everyone late today, she wondered where he was.

Malcolm arrived fifteen minutes later, the Saab driving in through the gate and into the garage that had originally been the stable. Martha and Deliah went inside, so that by the time he entered the kitchen everyone was around the table.

"You shouldn't leave the strimmer outside, it will rust," he said.

Martha put her hand to her mouth. "Of course," she said. "I'll put it away before dark."

Malcolm nodded sagely. "What are you reading now?" he asked Simon, who had scoffed his tea rapidly and got stuck into his book. Simon raised up the cover and Malcolm peered down to read - something or other by Chomsky. He sighed, exasperated to find his son reading something that he couldn't relate to. "Did we have any visitors?" he asked, sitting down for tea at last.

"No, why should we have?" said Martha, puzzled.

"Maybe, maybe not."

"You let the outbuilding didn't you?" She was referring to a converted barn on the fringe of the property that they had debated renting out for a while.

"As a matter of fact, yes."

"Malcolm!!" She stood up, upset.

"Now, now listen. What use is it really, if all we're using it for is storage?"

"But we are so happy here, with no one to bother us."

"Don't worry. This guy I've found is a recluse by all accounts. One of my clients recommended him - Vollet from the newspaper. The man is some kind of author, all he wants is peace and quiet to write."

"And how well does Vollett know him?"

"He's written some reviews for the paper I think."

"So, not very well."

"Martha .. the guy's a writer, not a motorcycle outlaw. And anyway, it's done. An extra grand a month, think about that." He mopped up his tea, and wiped his lips with a serviette.

There was silence for a while. "Dad, we lost one of the chickens," said Deliah.

"Which one?" he asked.

The 'writer' arrived on Saturday morning, just as they were preparing to drive to the supermarket. It was disconcerting, as he wasn't meant to be here for at least another week. They watched as the yellow Corsa pulled up outside the gate and the man got out. He was thick set with a thick orange beard and horn rimmed glasses, wearing a yellow turtleneck sweater with a blazer, trim jeans and high laced boots. He looked like a possible author. He inspected the farmhouse and then the outbuilding, without making any sort of greeting, just gesturing at Malcolm to open the gate.

"Well, that's damn inconvenient," murmured Malcolm. Nethertheless, he went over to meet the man. "Frank?" he asked, as he got near. The man nodded.

"Well, this is awkward," he said, "but we weren't expecting you till next week."

"But the place is available," said Frank.

"Yes, but hardly ready."

"Ah, in that case I'm sorry. It's possible I got my dates mixed up. How inconvenient is it?"

"It's just we've been using it for storage. There's a lot of stuff to be moved out of there."

"But it is furnished?"

"No, not at all."

Frank curled up his lip in disapproval. "But I especially asked for furnished lodgings, what do you expect me to do, fit furniture in the boot of my car?" he gestured towards the yellow vehicle.

"I'm sorry but you'll have to take that up with Vollett, he made no mention of that to me." Malcolm put his hands on his hips, to show that he was irritated.

"So where do I sleep, after driving all this way?"

"A hotel? By tomorrow we could have the place cleared .. I think. There's a folding bed in there, some other odds and sods of furniture you could use for the time being. That is the best we can do, considering the situation is hardly our fault."

"That's very accommodating yes. I don't mind helping clear the place if it comes to that. Perhaps with a bit of graft we could get it done before tonight even?" Frank peeped through his glasses hopefully. "I'm willing to put down an extra two months in advance plus the week early."

Malcolm considered this. "Well, we have something to take care of right now," he said, "but I'll see if I can put the boys onto it." He turned and strode back up to the house, where Martha was stood by the Saab watching apprehensively. In the meanwhile, Frank went and popped open his boot and took out two battered leather suitcases. It was all the luggage he seemed to have.

By the time they returned from the supermarket the work was well underway, and a pile of office furniture, skis, bicycle frames etc was stacked outside. Now there was the problem of where to put it. Some of it would have to be sold. Still, it looked like their guest would be able to move in today. They put away the shopping and when they got back outside, Frank and Oliver and Simon were walking towards the garden job complete. Deliah had gone upstairs.

"Fine boys you have here," said Frank. "College for you both isn't it?" They both nodded.

"Will you eat with us Frank?" asked Martha.

"No, I have imposed too much already. If you don't mind, I'll go up to my new accommodation and try to settle in." And without waiting for an objection, he turned again and went up to the barn. They all watched.

"So lads," Malcolm said to Oliver and Simon. "What did you talk about, you and our guest?"

"Nothing," said Oliver. "He hardly said anything."

"Nothing! Nothing at all?" Oliver shook his head.

"But he does have a nice speaking voice," said Martha.

"Except when he's annoyed. Did you hear that edge? Still, I suppose you have to expect writers to be a bit cranky."

"What's he going to eat though?" said Martha. "He can't have eaten all day, and he can't have much in his luggage."

"No," said Malcolm, "it's a bit strange." All the rest of that day, while they transferred the items they'd taken out of the barn into the house, cluttering up the study and garage, Frank failed to come out of the building. During the evening, watching television, Malcolm at intervals would go over to the patio doors and prise apart the blinds to peer out. The yellow car remained where it was, and about eight o clock a light appeared in the living room window, and then got turned off around ten. Simon was upstairs reading and Deliah was on her phone, while Oliver was out somewhere. Eventually he put it out of his mind and joined Martha in bed and fell asleep.

From his window, in the dark, Frank watched their bedroom light wink out. He opened the window and lit up a rolled cigarette. He watched the house for a long time. There was an empty packet of poppadoms at his feet.

In the morning Malcolm got up and went straight to the patio window. When he looked out the car had gone. He looked at the clock. It was barely eight! It wasn't until Oliver came down around midday that he got an answer. "Oh yeah", said Oliver, "he drove off around six."

"You saw him?"

"I was getting some water."

Malcolm fumed. Somehow it was irritating. "On a Sunday," he muttered. They spent the day sorting out the junk from the stuff they needed to keep.

"We've got this skiing gear that Brandon sent us," he said. "How on earth are we going to get rid of that?"

"You don't think the boys will want to take it with them, if they go to Berne next year?" said Martha.

"I doubt it. Hardly what you want to be seen in off piste is it? You'd have to be half-piste to wear the stuff actually .."

The Corsa reappeared about four pm, followed by a short white high topped truck. They both drove up to the barn, and while Frank got out of the car, a man in overalls left the lorry and walked round to the rear, unlocking and raising the shutter on its unit. The pair of them climbed in and began to pull out furniture - an iron frame bed, a desk, a table, a chest of drawers and two armchairs, all with the appearance of having come from a salvage yard. Once it was all out of the lorry, Frank gave Malcolm a wave and then him and the lorry driver carried it all into the barn. The driver left, and no one saw Frank for the rest of the day.

"See," said Frank that night as they were watching a talent contest on the television, "you wouldn't even know he was there. He's going to be no trouble at all."

The next day however he rang Vollet from the office and told him that the tenant he'd recommended had turned up early.

"Really?" said Vollet. "Was that a problem? I'm sure I gave him the right date."

"No doubt you did, he seems a bit ... what do you know about this guy, Vollet?"

"What do you need to know? He was a big deal about fifteen years ago with some postmodern novella, up for the .. not the Booker.. one of those other ones. Anyway, we were very proud of him. He used to be on the Gazette as staff - junior reporter, out of one of the universities near here."

"You remember him?"

"Barely. I was current affairs back then, and he will have been doing local interest, and anyway he didn't stay long. Some poems he'd written got picked up by the arty magazines and he went off to become a bohemian."

"So, what brought him back?"

"Failure I suppose. Everyone was waiting for the big novel and it never turned up. Did workshops, lecturing, got back in touch with us and we let him do local arts. Now he claims to have got the inspiration back and that's why I sent him to you. I mean, he must be doing alright, if he can front the rent, yes? Maybe he has an advance."

"Yes, that sounds right. I just wanted to be sure he wasn't a crank .. did you ever read his book?"

"Read it .. jesus .. I tried but it was all written from the perspective of different objects in a room or something, written from the perspective of the lampshade, yeah .. that's when I gave up."

Malcolm laughed. "Artists huh? Well, that explains a lot. I guess we'll just leave him to his own devices, see how we get on."

It was a whole month before Malcolm found his way into Frank's quarters and this was by Frank's own invitation. It was strange of course, because as landlord he really had the right to enter at any time, but there was something about his tenant's demeanour that made him feel as though this would be the most terrible intrusion. Even when Frank was absent, he shirked at the idea of opening up the barn to look around, in case his guest made an unexpected return. He had made some overtures, along the lines of - 'so you're a writer huh?' - but all this had brought was grunts of affirmation. Then October, as the rains started, Frank came over to the garden to complain about a leak in the roof. Malcolm at first was delighted, it would give him the chance to go into the dwelling at last and look around, but then of course fixing a roof could be expensive.

The barn had been divided into four high ceilinged rooms. Living quarters with adjoining kitchen, and then a small bedroom with an ensuite bathroom. In the living quarters the desk and table had been set up along with the armchairs: that were covered in some bobbly mustard coloured material, products of some indiscernible decade. Curtains had been hung up above the windows, plain dark blue, with no real attempt to coordinate the decor. In fact, the only 'style' came from the rooms original fittings - the laminate that had been laid down, the plastered walls and carefully retained wooden beams. Apart from that it was neat but spartan. There was a laptop on the desk, but as Malcolm knew no internet connection, and it was probably being used pretty much as a typewriter. He saw no pens or notebooks, no books! Nothing that spoke to him much about the writer at work. He peered into the kitchen. This too was neat, in fact Frank only seemed to own one pan. There was an open packet of crackers on the counter, but no apparent sign of cookery, no washing up next to the sink.

"The leak's in here," said Frank and went into the bedroom, so Malcolm mumbled an 'oh' and followed him. In here was the iron bed, with an incongruous pink mattress and the spare sheets and blankets they had given him. All his clothes must have been stuffed into the set of drawers somehow. His waxed coat was draped over the foot of the bedstead and two pairs of boots lay underneath it.

"There," said Frank and pointed to a corner of the ceiling. It was very high up. Malcolm squinted.

"Are you sure?" he said.

"Yes, right in the corner, look."

Malcolm squinted again. There was maybe some discolouration, or it may have been a shadow cast by one of the beams. "Well," he said doubtfully. "I can have someone take a look at the roof. Make sure there's not a problem." Martha's uncle Anthony would do it cheap he reckoned.

"That's all I ask," said Frank. There was a short silence. Malcolm pretended to study the corner some more. "Your garden's looking neat," said Frank.

"You think so?" said Malcolm mildly surprised. "We were thinking of having a vegetable patch next to the herb garden. Be a bit self sufficient, you know."

"It's a regular patch of paradise if you ask me."

"It is, it is! Although there's a bit of a problem with the public footpath, walkers seem to think they can cut across our drive. I'm in a dispute about it with the council. And we're slightly overlooked by the neighbours, but that won't be a problem once the hedge grows."

Frank went over to the window and looked out through the window at the 'neighbours' who were in fact separated by a whole field.

"Yes," said Malcolm, "those are the Davenports. Very well off. See the water feature .. imported. He's a magistrate I think, but I only know him to say hello to .."

"What about the house across the way?" asked Frank.

"That? Ah now, that actually is a farm, Mr .. Grayson. Very nice, very nice ... although a bit inconvenient sometimes, if he's herding his cattle and you get stuck behind them. There should be a way to get him to do it off peak or something, I mean we are meant to be a community here .."

Frank crinkled his eyes and smiled agreeably.

"Er .. yes well. I should go see what the children are up to, if you don't mind?" finished Malcolm. He looked up again at the corner. "You are sure, are you, about that leak?"

"Yes, just there, right in the corner." Frank pointed again, amused.

"I'll get someone to look at it of course." He left the barn and went out into the damp weather, shaking his head as though baffled. He was aware that he had gone in there to find out about his tenant, and instead told him all about himself.

The next day, when the weather had cleared, they were visited by Martha's mother Fiona. They were sat together in the living room, Deliah and Simon on the sofa and the adults perched on comfortable leather armchairs. It did not take long for conversation to turn to their new lodger.

"He's rather famous I hear," said Fiona.

"I'm not sure about famous," said Malcolm. "He did write a book once."

"A famous book though. What was it again?"

Malcolm tried to think. "Observation of the Tesseract," said Simon.

"What was that?" Malcolm remarked.

"Observation of the Tesseract by Frank Turlington, I got it online."

"You mean you read it?"

"Of course, yeah," said Simon, slightly bemused as to why you *wouldn't*, when you had the actual writer living at the bottom of your garden.

"So, what was it like?"

"It's quite good."

"Quite good! Woah! Rave review from Barry Norman there."

"I mean, it's very clever in sections, but I wasn't sure what the writer was trying to say," Simon mumbled shyly.

"Ah well, maybe that's because you're just not as smart as him, did you think about that?"

"Yes ..." Simon's voice tailed off.

"Anyway," said Fiona, "he would be an interesting person to invite to my salon, don't you think?"

"Oh, salon Fiona," Malcolm remarked, "you're not bloody French." The 'salons' had started not long after her father, Harold Puesch, had died of a stroke.

"But I could ask him."

"Well, he's out at the moment. Out most of the day usually. Comes back late in the afternoon with a half filled carrier bag. One thing I don't know if he's doing is actually writing ... and I'm not inviting him, don't ask me."

"I'll get Vollet to invite him, you're going to be awkward."

"I'm not being awkward, it's just the fellow hardly goes out of his way you know, to make himself sociable, and all you talk about there is politics anyway, he might not be interested."

"And then again he might. Not everyone sits on the fence like you do Malcolm."

"You don't sit on the fence so much as hop from one side to the other."

"Now you two, don't start," said Martha. At that moment the doorbell rang. Malcolm looked up confused, then said, "oh, that must be Anthony."

"Anthony?" said Fiona. The room felt her tense up.

"Yes sorry, I wanted him to look at a repair." He got up and went into the kitchen to answer the front door. Anthony was standing there in his worn Barbour coat and the battered van in the background. For some reason Malcolm took a certain pleasure in his company and garrulous ways, as long as it was for a limited period of time.

"Anthony, you old reprobate," he smiled.

"Malcolm, you merchant banker," Anthony guffawed, "and I don't mean that literally. That isn't my sister in law's car parked up is it?"

"I'm afraid so."

"Arghh damn it. Are you going to make me say hello?"

"Briefly, then we can say we need to look at the roof."

"Muddy boots. I can't come in, muddy boots."

"That's a good point, I'll bring her here." He went back to the room and brought back Fiona.

"Hey Fi!" said Anthony, expansively, "How's your mother doing?"

"She manages."

"I drove past the old plant on the way here. There's some firm from Vietnam making roller blinds or something."

"I'm glad someone found a use for it."

"And how are things with my brother?"

"Things are going fine, thanks."

"They must be yes, in your big new house"

"And Josie, do you see Josie?"

"Since she fucked off no, why should I? And then the kids too, good riddance I say. Now I just do what the fuck I want."

"Hmm, and Adie, is she alright in the care home?"

"Why don't you visit find out?"

"Peter always makes his visits, and he pays the bills."

"Aye well, Sylvester did his best, but then she needed full time care and he had the new missus and kids to look after."

"We've always been grateful to Sylvester."

"Good. Come on Malcy, let's go look at this barn." Then without further ceremony he tramped off to his van, and started to unload a ladder. Malcolm waited until Fiona had gone back into the room, then took a beer from the fridge and followed him. He waited until Anthony had the ladder propped against the barn then passed him the can. Anthony cracked open the can and took a swig with a sigh of satisfaction and handed it back.

"Better finish the rest when I come down," he said, "health and safety and all that. This is cash in hand, right?" Malcolm passed him a fold of notes which he tucked into his pocket. Properly motivated, he then ascended the ladder. Malcolm stood at the bottom. He surveyed his surroundings for a while - he was happy with them really, his own little bit of the country. He noted that the Davenports had visitors, the Palebys.

"Malcolm!" Anthony shouted from above. "There's nothing wrong with this fucking roof!"

Strangely enough, it was Martha who next succeeded in making inroads with their taciturn guest. Winter was starting to settle in and Malcolm was at work and she had the idea of taking over some leftover Sunday lunch to the barn. Frank, rather unusually, had not set off on his regular daily sojourn: perhaps dissuaded by the miserable weather. So, she took it upon herself to carry over a pot of excess curry and rice, hoisting the bright red casserole dish under one arm as she traipsed across the garden, hunched up against the driving rain. A regular size door had been built into the larger wooden double door of the barn - originally intended to allow the passing through of a haywain or later on: a tractor. She rang its electric bell and after some minutes, the smaller door creaked open and Frank's perturbed visage peered out. Not angry, just confused maybe: as to why anyone would elect to disturb him.

"We have some lunch leftover from yesterday," said Martha, "and it really is going to be just thrown away. I was wondering if you like curry."

Frank stared for a while, then broke into a gentle smile. "I do like curry, as it happens," he said, and drew open the door invitingly. Martha stepped into the living quarters, which were as spare as described to her by Malcolm, except they had been softened by the addition of a rug and a large anglepoise lamp. "It's just with it being so cold ..." she said.

"Here let me take that out of your hands," proffered Frank, carrying the pot over to the kitchen and lighting the stove. "You must have a glass of wine though, if I am to eat with a clear conscience." He swung open the fridge, which at a quick glance contained two bottles of wine, half a packet of butter and a tube of tomato puree.

"Oh .. just a small one then," said Martha, indicating a small measure between her finger and thumb, "it's a trifle early." He took two wine glasses from an overhanging cupboard.

"Is this working out for you then, the accommodation?" she asked.

"Oh yes," he said. "Just the right atmosphere, especially when I look out over the garden, denuded by the frost as it presently is."

"Do you like the garden, then?" she said, pleased.

"It is delicate, tranquil, like a winter puddle. I detect in it the feminine influence."

"It keeps me busy, during the summer that's true."

The bringing over of Sunday leftovers became part of the weekly routine over the rest of the winter, often accompanied by a midday glass of wine.

"We've been happy here really," Martha found herself saying one day, "and the children are a source of delight - worry too of course. Oliver being out all the time and it being hard to tell what he's up to, and Simon the other way, stays inside with his books and browsing, when they're not playing video games of course. Sometimes I wish I could mix them up a bit, you know? And Deliah is a worrier like me, comparing herself to those women in the magazines and internet. It's more difficult for girls these days in a lot of ways."

"Yes," said Frank, "it is."

"Aside from that I suppose we seem a bit dull. But my garden keeps me busy in summer and my embroidery in winter."

"Oh really, embroidery, I'd like to see that."

"You would?" she laughed, "I can't imagine why."

"I'm interested in anything creative."

"Oh, it's hardly creative, more of a hobby. My 'knitting' Malcolm calls it, to annoy me I suspect."

"But then Malcolm is a busy man."

"Oh, with his work and everything yes. I can't complain, it's his work paid for all this really. He does have his funny little ways though."

"Oh yes?"

"Well, you know. He gets irritated over little things, like someone putting his DVD collection out of order, or the garden tools being left out, but he's a good and kind person at heart, despite his attempts to act blaise and clever."

"Yes, but in that he is symptomatic of this town, isn't he?"

"What do you mean?"

"Just an observation, coming from the salon of your mother that I attended."

"Oh yes, how did that go? We were worried that it wouldn't be your thing at all."

"It was interesting in its way, but more for what it left out than what it included. Very much talk of business and politics and money, but little of the arts or culture, and isn't that what makes a place really, Martha?"

"Oh yes, yes! It must be."

"Your mother agreed to some extent, that space should be put aside for a creative hub, and sensitive people should be found to organise it."

"Like who?"

"Like you for instance."

"Me?! Oh gosh no, I'm not creative in the slightest."

"Oh no? What about your embroidery?"

"That? but you could hardly call that art.."

"Well, I think the creators of the Bayeux tapestry would disagree with you there Martha. And besides textile art is seen in a whole new light nowadays, it's not looked down upon just because it is the province of the feminine."

"I see."

"Anyway, you seem to me a natural choice."

"I'd .. I don't know, I'd have to think about it."

"Try talking with your mother, she'd be able to put you in touch with people who could organise the funding."

"Really, you really think so?"

"Martha, I do."

Martha left the barn feeling somehow lighter in spirit, frivolous, maybe even younger. Maybe she was tipsy. She had to resist the temptation to skip across the garden as she returned to the house.

"You're never at home anymore," said Malcolm. By now it was Spring and the buds on the apple tree were appearing and the daffodils were coming up. "I come back from work and things are all over the place, nothing's been done." He ran a finger along the sideboard as he spoke and raised it to look at the dust. "Already I've spent two hours this morning sorting out the laundry, and this is on my weekend."

"Then the children will have to do their bit, that's all. The boys when they're not at college. We've been spoiling them."

"Oh, I can imagine what sort of a job they'll do. One hardly comes home at all, and the other can't keep his nose out of a book. And Simon is Frank's friend now too, I saw them wandering one of the lanes together, discussing, well .. who knows what pretentious matters. And what is it you're doing at this 'hub' anyway, what is it that's so vital?"

"We're contributing to the spirit of the town, we're providing it with culture."

"You mean with your macrame workshops and watercolour sessions. Bit delusional don't you think?"

"That's right be snide, look down on me, just like you've got used to doing."

"Martha, I don't look down on you...you've raised three wonderful children ..."

"And that's all, that's all you see me as anymore. You don't remember that I had a spirit . .that I was youthful. We don't even go out," she sobbed.

"But that's because you said you felt safe here, secure .. you preferred it at home."

"I thought I did, but now I've been shown something else."

"Oh, by 'Frank'. Well, it's alright for him isn't it, making his money daydreaming and then going for a walk ... I don't even know what he does to be honest. I certainly don't see evidence of any writing."

"He's an influence."

"Oh, he's an influence, well .. that must be what it says on his passport under occupation. I am an influence .. "

"There you go, being facetious, you find that very easy, don't you?"

They heard the kids stir upstairs and instinctively hushed their argument.

"Let's leave this for now," said Malcolm.

"Fine, but I'm going to see my mother."

The Creative Hub took place in a disused community centre on the fringes of one of the town's more respectable neighbourhoods. At first, Martha had hoped that Fiona would take up a position on its board of directors, but she had declined, saying that would make it look far too much like a family enterprise, and might actively discourage investment. Instead, she recommended the wife of their neighbour, Mrs Davenport and her friend Mrs Paleby, who had experience of accounts. There was the rent on the building of course, and then the decision to renovate the interior, which required all kinds of outlay and permissions. This Martha took charge of, surprising herself with the adeptness with which she negotiated the maze of forms and approvals and the confidence she acquired in dealing with the various officials. Then there was the funding, for which they all campaigned and lobbied, but the raising of which proved to be Sheena Davenports arena of expertise, or at least she was the best connected. A consultant was brought in to advise on the renovations, to give them a fresh modern feel, and although this pushed up the expenses, Martha was able to make up the slight shortfall in cash with some of her savings. Everyone was impressed with the results. The interior was vibrant, with an open space for workshops and a lecture stage on one end and then a smaller, more informal social, 'coffee drinking' space marked by funky colourful furniture and bookshelves. There was a grand opening, at which local dignitaries, even the mayor, were present, although somehow the mayor's speech and its coverage in the Gazette managed to put Mrs Paleby's nose out of joint, as she felt it handed credit for the enterprise entirely to Martha and Sheena and overlooked her own contribution. After this she became far more lackadaisical in her handling of the finances.

It was mid May and Malcolm was staring out of the window one Sunday afternoon, drying some dishes, when Frank's Corsa chugged its way through the gate and pulled up outside the barn. He noticed at once there were a few people inside. As he carefully stacked the plate he'd been drying, Frank got out of the driver's seat and then two other people exited the car - a woman in her thirties with dyed purple hair and a thin bony man of indiscernible age with a shaved head wearing a camouflage jacket. Somehow Malcolm wanted to ignore their arrival, but felt really that he couldn't, so he went to the back door and opened it, giving a casual but stern wave to the newcomers, the tea towel in his other hand. Frank crossed the garden and came over, stopping about halfway.

"My sister and her friend," he said. "Stopping with me for a while. Your wife knows about it."

"She does?" Malcolm replied. "She didn't say anything."

"Well, I mentioned it as a possibility. That they'd be able to help her with the hub. And it's entirely within my rights as tenant. I've checked."

"Yes, it is, bearing in mind the limits of the lease ..." He wrung the tea towel unconsciously.

"I'll bring them over later. I thought we could have a get together in the garden, it being quite a nice day and all. I'll bring some samosas and a few bevvies."

"Well, that's appreciated b.."

"Agreed!! We'll be over later, and don't worry. My sister's very creative, she'll be able to help Martha out a lot."

Malcolm frowned as Frank turned his back and went over to the car. He stepped back inside, flung down the tea towel and went to the foot of the stairs. "MArtha!" he called out. She appeared on the landing, half her face still covered in moisturiser.

"Why are you shouting?" she said, annoyed.

"Frank's bloody sister's turned up."

"Has she? Yes, he said she might."

"But you didn't tell me?"

"I didn't think it would be for a while, and I knew you'd start making a big deal about it."

"Of course it's a big deal. I've got a bloody commune being set up at the bottom of my garden."

"Well, you wanted a tenant ..."

Deliah opened her bedroom door and stuck her head and shoulders out distressed. "You two aren't arguing again are you?" she asked.

"We're not arguing dear," said Martha, "We're just .. trying to reach an agreement about something."

"God Dad, why can't you let mum be happy?"

"Oh .. so that's the consensus is it? Well everyone, it's samosas and bevvies at four if you're interested. Why don't you invite your friends?" Deliah just went back inside and slammed her door.

"Look Malcolm, they've just come to help. It's like you said yourself - macrame and watercolours are a bit provincial, but these are proper artists, they're going to show us new and exciting things."

"You think so?"

Martha nodded enthusiastically. Malcom stepped back, defeated for the moment.

Out in the garden, among the newly flowering nasturtiums and delphiniums, they were watching a video of Frank's sister Olympia on the laptop, doing one of her performance pieces in what seemed to be a sparsely attended basement club in Camden, London. She was dressed in a purple leotard, to which had been stuck paper plates smeared in various colour paints. Weird arabic tinged music was playing in the background and she affected to be in some form of trance, moving in spasmodic, jerky movements to the Locrian scale and then during the musical lulls emitting a great howling scream and launching herself at the tautly stretched fabrics that were fashioned into a boundary around her, leaving them splattered with ovular crushed paint daubs and splatters in various colours.

"You see," said Frank, "how non-traditionality is the point." The chickens were clucking in their coop, down by the side of the house.

Martha looked fascinated. "Yes, it's just having the bravery to let yourself go, isn't it?" Malcolm was aware that he was expected to be sceptical, and so tried to avoid looking sceptical. Only Oliver was smirking, while Simon stayed quiet - not wanting to say that the idea seemed actually very shopworn and lazy by now - and Deliah was politely interested.

"And you Terence," Malcolm said, addressing the shaved headed man, "what is your oeuvre?"

"I paint," said Terence.

"Care to expand?"

"No."

Oliver picked up a samosa and munched on it, enjoying himself.

"Well," said Malcolm, feeling the need to try again. "Are we to expect a performance like this at the hub?"

Deliah's mouth dropped in horror. "Oh please mum, tell me you're not going to do something like that?"

Martha laughed. "No, I would just be involved in the organisation. I think a performance like that needs to be done by trained professionals."

"And how much training have you had, over the years Olympia?" said Frank slyly.

She ignored him. "It is more a matter of spirit than training," she said, "I believe that firmly." Terence nodded.

"And you manage to make a living from this ... art?" asked Malcolm.

"We make an art of living," said Olympia. This was somehow impressive to all.

"And the book Frank, how is that coming along?"

"Very good, I think I have a title."

Oliver coughed, stifling a laugh, and took a drink from the can of lager he'd been given.

"A title, gosh .. well, that's something. Care to share?"

Frank shook his head, "No," he said. All the children were trying not to laugh now. Deliah punched Simon's arm as he looked over trying to provoke her.

"Lovely night," said Frank, taking a sip of his own beer, and leaning back in the chair content, and it was nice, with the birds chirping in the trees and the scent of flowers and the blue sky with a hint of pink on the horizon. Only somewhere in the distance was there the churning of a tractor.

For the next few days, the peculiar guests provided the children with the source of their jokes. Oliver would ask Simon if he had finished his essay, and Simon would reply no but he had a title, while Deliah in turn would declare that she was not just lying in bed but making an art of living. Martha though, found herself getting on with the guests marvellously, and not just her but Sheena and other members of the Hub got into the habit of joining them in the garden for lively afternoons soirees, during which Frank or Olympia would play host, regaling them with tales of the artistic life. Word seemed also to have got out about the drive being a public right of way, and often, returning from work Malcolm would have to sound his horn in order to clear some stray creatives from his path and get into the converted stable. Then his mood already spoiled he would go into the untidy house, the standards of which he had long since stopped trying to uphold, take a plate of whatever cuisine, intended for the guests, was cluttering the kitchen and sequester himself in the living room, which was the only tidy room in the house and turn on the tv so that the natter outside was drowned out. The children had learned to accept this, but by a process of osmosis were driven, when not otherwise occupied, to join the proceedings outside where they began to find the trio entertaining and at times even informative.

"Malcolm doesn't join us though," Sheena said to Martha, on one particularly pleasant summer evening, where they were making a watercolour study of the rose bed. Deliah's mp3 player had been borrowed and an improvised dance session, led by Olympia, was taking place on the lawn behind them, observed by Frank and Terence as they sipped beer and ate from packets of crisps.

"Tssk," said Martha. "All he does now is stay in the house and mutter and get under everyone's feet. And he's become stingy. For years you know he never let me out of the house, and now I've found freedom he's cut off the money. Says if I want something go to the Hub, that if people wanted our art they would be willing to pay for it."

"Such an ignorant attitude."

"He's taken charge of the groceries and only buys the bare minimum. The poor kids are coming out here just to get fed properly. Fortunately we have all that equipment we brought out of storage I was able to put on ebuy, even the stuff he said he wanted to keep. I don't think he's noticed that its .. dwindling."

"And the performance, are we ready for the performance?" Sheena was referring to the embroidered backdrop they had been working on for the past two months. It was indeed a voluptuous creation of which they were rightly proud, for how many people could have fulfilled the brief given to them by Olympia, that it should exemplify the Spirit of the Goddess within every woman. After the performance there was going to be the highlight of the evening, when Frank would read excerpts from his upcoming novel. There was a great excitement about this in literary circles and it was certain to bring attention to the town, for intelligentsia from across the country and even abroad were preparing to travel and report upon this unanticipated event. It seemed like Martha's efforts in setting up the Hub had been validated after all. What is more, her own creation would be hanging in the background, seen and noted by all concerned. She felt splendid, filled with a powerful new spirit.

There was only one problem, as Olympia discreetly explained a few days later, and that was an unfortunate remnant from Frank's past, certain improprieties that had occurred in the wellbeing room during his time as guest lecturer at a mid ranking university. In fact, it could be said that Frank had not just come up here to write, but to escape the ugly rumours that were following him. And these were all exaggerated of course. In fact the women concerned had probably come onto him, and then the matter blown out of proportion by bitter rivals. All the same, a blackmailer had found them and was threatening to send copies of the complaints to the Gazette, just ahead of the grand event. It would be completely ruined, in fact it would probably have to be abandoned, and the existence of the Hub itself would be brought into question. Martha was angry, these people always spoiled things.

"Yes," said Olympia, "it's true, they always try to destroy the creative spirit." They were sat in the kitchen.

"What is it they want?"

"Five thousand pounds I'm afraid."

"And that's this once, later they will want more I suppose."

"Martha. That is Frank's problem. What I am thinking of is the performance, that it not be spoiled. Otherwise, I wouldn't ask. One payment, so the event not be ruined, then Frank will have to deal with his own messes. It shouldn't be a problem once publishers start bidding on his book."

"And Frank can't pay this individual himself? He seems to manage the rent okay."

"That money is virtually gone. We're managing the rent between the three of us, and that's with Terence on the sofa and me on the fold up. Believe me things have become very cramped, but I stay to help out my brother."

"I see. Well, we have banked the rent and I could get access to the account, but if Malcolm saw that it was gone .."

"We'll replace it, as soon as Frank gets money for the book, I promise."

Malcolm spent the following Sunday angrily picking up discarded dog ends from the lawn and removing abandoned crisp packets from amongst the foxgloves in the herbaceous borders. The recycling box he saw was already full of empty wine bottles and lager cans, not to mention takeaway boxes. At nights he would ask Martha if she was having a good time and she would reply yes, not seeming to notice the pointed sarcasm. She had even started to ask about the boys' rooms, whether Olympia and Terence might make use of them once

Oliver and Simon started university, seeing as the trio were living in such stifled conditions together up at the barn.

"And what about Deliah?" he asked.

"What do you mean?"

"How safe would she be, with those two here?"

"Oh, really Malcolm, that's just like you to imagine such terrible things." All the same, the matter of Frank's past improprieties did cross her mind. "And we'll be here anyway. And it's only until the performance," she added, "then the whole lot of them will be on their way."

"That means renewing the lease, it's out of the question."

"You're not going to throw them out, before the event?"

"I'll draw up a special contract, giving them the extra month, then they're gone."

"Well, won't that look surly."

"Really, you want them to stay so much?"

She was thinking of the big empty house once the boys had gone, Deliah soon enough finishing school. Marital relations between her and Malcolm had not taken place for a few months. But once the Hub was a success, they could come together again, maybe even Malcolm dealing with the accounts, if he stopped being stubborn about it all. Of course, she'd have to square the missing cash first.

"No, but don't upset them, not before the performance. Please. This is one thing I ask, then things will become more normal."

"You promise?"

"I promise."

The following weekend there was another party, this one going on into the night. Malcolm didn't join in, he just stayed in the sitting room and turned up the volume on the tv, trying to smother the sound of music and laughter.

Outside, near the driveway, Fiona was making her farewells to Martha as her husband Peter waited impatiently in the nearby car.

"It's a shame Malcolm couldn't be persuaded to come out," she said, "are you sure he's alright?"

"Oh yes," Martha replies, "he's just having a professional sulk, because he sees what a success we're having out here." She turned to look around at the groups who were visible in the glow of the candles arrayed on the outside tables, yellow light flickering off the underside of the apple tree and the rowans. The Davenports were still here, as were members of the Grayson family, mingling with the group of locally frustrated creatives who were gathered hopefully around Frank, as though some of the meagre notoriety he'd garnered might rub off on them. "Even our very own neighbours have been brought closer together, never mind the townfolk," she added stridently.

"You should be proud," said Fiona, "and so should Malcolm if he had any sense."

Snatches of Frank's conversation drifted over ... "then he said, there must be a way to make these cows move faster" .. and everyone around him laughed uproariously. Deliah was with a small group of friends, and rather ridiculously Olympia was trying to drunkenly impress them, chattering endlessly while they exchanged half mortified expressions, coughing suppressed laughter into their hands. Simon was talking shyly to two young students from a nearby university, which was good to see. It gave the hope that he would make new friends when he left home. There were a few absentees, Oliver out with friends, making the most of things before he left for university himself, Terence somewhere in town apparently, but overall it was a healthy cross section of local culture, brought together and coalescing in her very own garden.

"Well, well, well," said Anthony, "you said you were coming but I wasn't sure. Come in." He waved Simon and Oliver off the doorstep and into his hallway. "Sorry about the mess. I had a cleaner but she left." He chuckled mirthlessly to himself. The hallway was cluttered with a half fixed bike and shopping bags that had yet to be taken into the kitchen - from which the faint sweet smell of garbage emanated. The front room was messier: uncleared plates, full ashtrays and empty lager cans, torn rizla packets and more shopping bags, these filled with bundles of wiring and other items for the scrap merchant. Anthony searched around until he found three cans of unopened beer still bound together by their plastic rings. He pulled one loose and offered it towards the boys. Simon shook his head but Oliver reached forward and took it, not wanting to seem rude. Anthony winked and pulled one loose for himself, listening for the crack and hiss as he opened the ring pull and then taking a satisfied swig. Then he cleared a space on the sofa and sat down.

"So, you're worried about dad," he said. "That's what you told me on the phone."

Oliver tried to perch casually on the arm of a nearby chair. "Yes, he doesn't seem right," he said, "but there isn't really anyone we can go to about it."

"Except Great Uncle Anthony, eh?"

"Well, dad sort of likes you, and you're not .."

"Not what?"

"Part of mum and dad's crowd," said Simon, "you can see it better."

"Ahhh, bring a fresh pair of eyes to the situation, eh?"

"Exactly."

Anthony took another long gulp of lager then, with his arms along the back of the sofa, took some time to mull things over, his pose expressing a certain sense of gratification at being asked to solve the problem. "Well, I can tell you one thing right off the bat," he said, "and that's your artist friends are taking the piss out of you."

"How .. how do you know that?" asked Oliver

"The baldy one's .. started coming into the Lion to buy his amphetamine. Gets a bit chatty too, once he's had a snort."

"Right, and what's he been saying?"

"What a joke this Hub is. How it's only worth it for the fanny, the odd repressed daughter that gets dragged in there. An over optimistic art student if you're lucky. What they're really after is the funding, or a healthy slice of it anyway. Do some bollocks and call it art, like these fucktards are going to know anyway. I reckon that's the way he expressed it." He sipped again.

Oliver and Simon deliberated this awkwardly, staring at their feet.

"The only one might be serious is this Frank. I mean he's got an eye out for skirt and moolah too, but baldy reckons there's another motive as well."

Oliver looked up "Like what?" he asked.

"Disruption," said Anthony.

"The only thing is, we tell mum this we don't know if she's going to listen, she's too involved."

"And your dad tells it, she's going to reckon its lies."

"Right." Oliver looked towards Simon. "You used to talk to him, didn't you? What about?"

"Frank?" Simon replied.

"Yeah."

"Books. The dissolution of reality, that kind of thing. He introduced me to Baudrillard"

"Mate of his?" asked Anthony.

"Er .. not exactly."

"Well ... let's go talk to Malcy anyway. I mean, he works with money yeah? These fuckers are fiddling things he should be able to figure it out."

"That's right," said Mrs Paleby. "I left the Hub two months ago. First, they took me off the accounting, then they were very dismissive about my attempts at decoupage. It was the last straw." She was sat with Malcolm in a small coffee shop just down from his office. Malcolm was wan, slightly unshaven and at work they had begun to talk about him. His performance was down, he seemed distracted, several times he might be caught just staring out of a window. One of the directors had asked him if he needed to take some time out, deal with problems at home. He had shuddered, that was the last thing he wanted to do, and for while he sharpened up his concentration, but two days later the sense of mental abstraction had overtaken him again. Now though he was focused, having yesterday checked the personal accounts - five thousand out last week and in again yesterday, with no explanation. His wife's savings poured into the Hub with just a few hundred pounds left. That meant their mortgage rates ever went up they were probably screwed.

"So, who's dealing with the books now?" he asked.

"No one as far as I know. If an auditor gets in there, he's going to have a field day. I think Martha's relying on her parents to make sure that doesn't happen."

"Can she do that. Rely on them?"

"It depends. How worried they are about their political opponents finding out and stirring up the doodoo. The Hub though, probably who cares? Now, if they were mismanaging a children's hospital ... "

"Yes, I understand."

They discussed what Mrs Paleby had said as Malcolm drove the boys to the railway station, all their luggage in the boot in preparation for their first year in halls. Martha had started crying as they left of course, embracing them before they got into the car, and even Deliah had been emotional about it. It had been a genuinely moving moment and all of a sudden they were a close knit family again. The wind had been blowing the harvested remains of the crops in the fields across the road and somehow it brought to mind the feeling of christmases and birthdays.

"Once this performance is done, I'll get them to leave then try to get into the Hub's finances, sort it out myself," said Malcolm as he concentrated on negotiating a roundabout.

Simon was subdued while Oliver looked out of the window, with the strange feeling that he shouldn't be going, not just yet.

"If you have any trouble with them, let us know, I'll come back," he said.

Malcolm made a self conscious chuckle and looked at them in the rear view mirror. "Think I can't handle it do you?" he asked.

"Just if you need a hand," said Oliver.

"Don't worry about that boys. Just you get settled in. The law is on my side here. If I want them to leave, they have to leave and that's all there is to it." He squinted ahead as they made the turn off for the town centre. He had this awful feeling, with the boys gone, there were less people 'on his side', but he couldn't confess openly to this of course. He concentrated on overtaking a Subaru that was dawdling in front of them and making it to the station in time. Soon enough they were parked before its Victorian facade, fluted columns and pilasters supporting its ornately carved architrave, unloading the luggage from the boot.

"Well, I don't suppose I need to tell you to have a good time," said Malcolm. "Just try and do some studying too, eh lads? In between all the beer. And by study I mean the books they tell you to read Simon, not the ones that caught your eye in the local library."

"I'll try," said Simon. He flushed slightly, thinking of the Selby Junior he'd brought to read on the way down.

Malcolm put a hand on his shoulder and squeezed it. "I know you will," he said. He realised he was in danger of crying suddenly himself, not just a sob but a wail. He shook his head and settled for a moist eye. "I know you will. Both you boys are going to get on fine, that's the Hinchcliffe way."

"One more month?" said Frank. They were out in the garden. It was very much like it had been a year ago, except the grass was more worn, with so many people using the lawn and the weeding had been neglected and with so many flowers come and gone, the plants needed deadheading. Realising that any investigation into the Hub could only implicate his wife, he now aimed to get rid of his tenants as fast as was expedient for all concerned.

"Yes, enough for this grand performance," he said, "and then .. I'm afraid we need to use the barn again."

"So, it's not because we've offended you, Malcolm?"

"No, it's purely practical considerations. I'll be taking some time off work .. and after that I'll need to use the barn for ... projects." He did not mention that the real reason for his taking time off work was to keep a watch over things, now the boys were leaving.

"Projects, that's interesting. What sort of projects Malcolm?"

"I was thinking of .. building a boat, be a bit creative like my wife."

"A boat, so you like sailing then?"

"I ..I don't know. I figured I'd build the boat and then maybe give it a go, yes?"

"Well, really I'd suggest you do it the other way round. Be a shame to build the boat and then find out you didn't like sailing, wouldn't it?"

"Maybe I could sell it?"

"Are you asking me Malcolm?"

"I .. I.."

"Maybe you need to think about it some more. Never mind. It's probably a good idea to take this time off and get your head together a bit. Everyone's noticed you've been acting a bit strange."

"What do you mean?"

"Isolated .. you've become isolated Malcolm. Probably a bit paranoid. I wish you'd participate more, it would do you good."

"Participate how?"

"Probably .. Olympia is the one to talk to there, she's the one who's done the whole mental wellbeing thing. In the meantime, we'll keep it quiet round here, try to give you some peace of mind."

"Right, thank you." It seemed best to play along a bit, then when the lease ended, serve the eviction anyway. What were they going to do about it?

Malcolm was alone in the house. With the date of the performance - and Franks reading - getting nearer, the Hub and to a lesser extent the town was in a state of increased anticipation. Martha was there most days now, overseeing the preparations and many of the ladies she worked with were getting giddy. For the umpteenth time that day he peered through the blinds out across the garden. Frank was there! Worse, he was talking to the Davenports, Sheena and Charles. They talked, their faces expressing some sort of concern, Frank pointed at his own head, then looked over at the house. Quickly, Malcolm withdrew the hand that was parting slightly the blind and stepped backwards, terrified of being noticed. Had they seen the blind move? Now they would think he was paranoid, he had to exert more control. It took a massive effort of will, but he determined to go out on the patio and act normal. So, he put on a cardigan and his gardening shoes and went to feed the chickens. He brought out the chicken feed from the garage and waved confidently to the Davenports as he moved round the side of the house to the coop. He opened it up, poured out some feed and watched them peck around for a bit. Then he herded the chickens back in, returned the feed, went into the sitting room and sat down. The whole endeavour had been exhausting. He laid his head back and looked at the ceiling sweating, breathing deeply to control his nerves. Later he went out to do some weeding. The Davenports had gone back inside. He cleared one of the borders and felt a bit better. Deliah came back from school.

"Hi dad!" she said, in a tone that was overly bright and artificial, trying too hard. She came over. "Busy?"

"Just tidying up the border. How is school?"

"It's okay I suppose." Actually, all anyone asked her about now were her tenants, and the various bits of gossip her friend's parents had attached to them. She was fed up of it.

"Ah 'okay I suppose', a typical teenager response." They both smiled. It had been a while since he'd been snarky.

"Got homework?" he asked.

"Yes, of course."

"Want some help?" He stood up and shook the dirt off his gardening gloves. Deliah looked surprised but said, "Yes, okay sure."

When Martha eventually got back, having been loaned the car now Malcolm was off work, she found them together in the kitchen, with the homework set to one side and giggling together as they played something on her phone.

"Get 'im, get i'm!" Malcolm was shouting. She scowled. Having Malcolm at home was just irritating.

"What are you doing?" she asked.

"Playing a game!" yelled Malcolm, "It's called Funky Lizard ... Get IM!" Deliah giggled, while Martha grimaced and shook her head in exasperation. She put away her bag of art materials and returned to the kitchen and looked in the fridge. "You didn't go shopping?" she asked.

"No," he said, "I'm going to order pizza." He put down the game. "Sorry, how was the Hub?"

"Fine, thank you for asking."

"Ready for the performance?"

Martha shrugged and went out of the room. Deliah and Malcolm looked at each other. "I'll go," said Deliah with a sigh and she followed her mother upstairs. Malcolm contemplated matters for a moment, wrinkled up his face, tried playing Funky Lizard again, then put the game down realising he wasn't interested in it at all.

The next morning, conscience pricked slightly by Martha's comments, he took a walk down to the village grocer. They were sleeping separately now, him occupying Oliver's old room. No doubt Deliah had noticed and it worried her, but he still felt the marriage would be pulled back together, once the lousy interlopers were out of the way. It was a very pleasant walk, despite the grey sky and a light drizzle, along the country lanes looking at the fields - turned over now, ploughed soil with the stubble of the harvested wheat and the shorn roots of beet sticking out - and he wondered why he didn't make the journey more often. In the grocers he picked up some basics - fresh veg, pasta, rice, bread and contemplated going to the butchers for some choice cuts. Maybe doing a bit of cooking. There was a small queue at the till, the old lady in front of him chatting to the woman behind the counter. He tssked slightly.

"Can't these cows move any faster?" said the man behind him, one of a trio of workmen from the local lumberyard, and there was some snorting laughter. Malcolm chuckled as well, although the joke was slightly bizarre. The old lady smiled at him and moved away, and he paid for his goods and went to the butchers. Then he walked home but for some reason his mood started to turn sour. He couldn't escape the feeling that somehow the people in the shop had been laughing at *him*.

"Shopping Malcolm?" said Frank, as he walked through the gate. He was still lost in his worries so Frank's comment surprised him, he hadn't even noticed he was there.

"Shopping?" He looked down at the bag. "Oh yes, shopping!" he smiled brightly and held it up.

"That's right Malcolm, you have shopping!" said Frank in a strange way, as though dealing with a simpleton. "My sister is here by the way, she wanted to show you something."

"Mmhh," he thought about it. "I'll just put this away."

"Yes, I'll send her over."

Olympia entered the kitchen just as he was putting the last of the rice into a cupboard. She was carrying a woven basket.

"So you want us to help you?" she asked.

"Do I?"

"You wanted to participate, feel part of things."

"Oh yes .. maybe."

"Don't worry, this will be painless. You might even go away thinking it's a load of hippy nonsense but that's okay. The least thing is, you can say you gave it a go."

"Okay, once."

"Great, great." She reached into the basket and pulled out a quartz crystal. "Now, don't groan," she said, but Malcolm couldn't help it, he groaned involuntarily.

"Never mind. Now I'm going to make us some Japanese tea and you're going to look at the crystal and write down ten relaxing things it makes you think of and then go for a walk and see if you find the world any different. How about that?"

Well, it was nonsense he thought, but sounded painless as promised. He held out his arms, palms upwards in a conciliatory gesture and said okay. Olympia left Malcolm looking at the crystal and went over to the kitchen counter to brew the tea. She turned on the kettle, found a cup and then took out a packet of teabags, the ones she'd soaked in mescaline and waited for the water to boil.

Charles Davenport was in his study, reading through some affidavits, when he glanced up and saw, through the bay window, Malcolm standing in the front garden looking at the fountain. At first, he thought he must have paused there on his way up to the house, but no, he was just stood there staring at it. The darnedest thing! He better go and see what was up. He sighed, put down the forms he'd been studying and went down the hallway to the backdoor, exchanging his indoor slippers for his garden slippers. When he opened the door and got outside, Malcolm was still there. His expression was strange, fixed in a sort of eerie rapture as he gazed at the falling water, following the patterns it made.

"Are you alright Malcolm?" he asked.

Malcolm didn't answer for a considerable number of moments. Eventually he said, "Lovellly, lovely fountain," in a peculiar stretched out drawl.

Charles kept a careful distance. "Yes, Malcolm, it is a nice fountain," he replied.

"You have the bessst fountain in the worrrld."

"Well, I wouldn't quite say that."

"Lovvlelly." He turned towards Charles and grinned. There was a sheen to his complexion, like it had been rubbed with glass.

"It is nice." Charles stepped backwards, "Was there something you wanted?" he asked.

Malcolm shook his head lazily. "Noo," he drawled. "I might listen to the birds. They are my friend."

"Oh yes, the birds are everyone's friend."

"Nice birds."

"Nice birds," Charles agreed. He had been walking backwards steadily and was almost back at the door. To his relief he watched Malcolm walk out of the gate back onto the road. "Sheena!!" he called once he got inside.

"What is it?" she asked, coming out of the kitchen with an oven glove still on.

"It's that Malcolm, he's gone stark bonkers, just like people have been saying. I think the bloody chap might need to be sectioned."

Malcolm found the experience of the crystal so revelatory he was keen to try it again two days later. By then everyone else was busy, it being the night of the reading. The town was suffering from an unusual influx of intelligentsia - high brow critics, publishers, several well known writers from both the British Isles and the continent, most of them being put up at the hotel next to the railway station: so for that week, the pubs and cafes around that area became places to avoid. Anyway, not really wanting to supervise the procedure more than once, Olympia had left Malcolm with the crystal and a handful of teabags in a plastic sachet, tucked into the corner of a cupboard. She had other things to think about by this time, the performance and the money she'd got from Martha. Three grand had gone to Frank's blackmailer - who was real enough - but she'd pocketed the extra two herself. Half would go towards appeasing the debt collectors she'd left behind, the rest she'd put towards a holiday in the Maldives. Fuck it, after putting up with this tedious bullshit all summer, she reckoned it was well earned...

 This time Malcolm caught the attention of several more locals as he wandered along the lanes. It was Mr Grayson who spotted him in one of the fields dancing around in a circle. He brought his tractor to a halt and stood up, leaning out slightly to get a proper view. He saw that Charles Davenport was standing in one of the nearby lanes, observing Malcolm also. He left the tractor and strolled over. Davenport had been carefully monitoring Malcolm ever since the fountain episode.

"What's that all about?" asked Grayson.

"Fellows snapped," said Davenport. "That's all there is to it."

They watched for a while. Malcolm had his arms outstretched and was spinning around, then hopping.

"I didn't like to say," said Grayson, "but there was something odd about the way he kept himself shut up, while we were all hobnobbing in the garden."

"Not that Martha was too bothered, very happy with her art friends."

"Aye something going on there, I wouldn't be surprised. She was over to that barn with some hotpot once a week."

"Hotpot was it?"

"Aye."

Charles shook his head. "It's a damn shame," he said.

When Deliah got home from school, her father was sat cross legged on the ground to the side of the house, facing the chicken coop. The doors were open, and there were only two hens and a cockerel strutting around nearby. The rest must have absconded somewhere. He was watching the cockerel avidly. It really was marvellous, with its downy coat of black feathers speckled tawny brown and the red crown on its head as it wandered around bobbing imperiously. It had been a shame to keep it cooped up. The loss of the other birds troubled him though. "They went," he said as she approached, "the hens. I'm not sure why."

"Dad."

He turned his head to look at her. There was the sound of a problem in her voice.

"What?" he asked, concerned. The mescaline was leaving his system, so he felt thinned out but very clear.

"There's a problem at school." She looked anxious.

He stood up quickly, dusting down his trousers. "Problem, what sort of problem?"

"Clara."

"Who's she?"

"My friend, with the fringe."

"Why is that a problem?"

"It's not .... its .." She was biting the inside of her cheek.

"Deliah, come on."

"She got expelled. It's those friends of mum's fault."

"Why, what did they do?" He was alert and attentive very quickly.

"Gave her drugs," Deliah sort of mumbled.

"WHAt??"

"I think they gave her drugs and school found them in her bag."

"Here?"

Deliah shook her head. "At the Hub I think .. Olympia said she could show her some dance moves .. and then Terence turned up and .. "

Malcolm was aware that he was becoming intensely angry, like something boiling up, like something coming up through a vent.

"And what .. did something happen?"

Deliah nodded, crying.

Malcolm's face tightened and became darker. "Right," he said. "Right ..." He started over to the barn.

"Dad," said Deliah. He turned around. "They're not there." He looked at her confused. "It's the performance," she said. "We were meant to be getting ready."

He considered this for a while, his face blinking with the effort.

"Right, yes," he said. "Put something on, whatever you've got."

"Are we going?"

He nodded grimly, searching his pockets for his car keys. Martha had the car. Then looking for his phone. He'd left it on the kitchen table. "We'll get a taxi," he said.

Deliah watched him, she wanted to ask again about Carla, but somehow, she daren't. Instead she just said, "Okay."

Vollet looked around the crowd. The Hub was busy, that was for certain. Friends and family of the members, that you'd expect, but then curious onlookers too, and the imported intellectuals. Oh, and some local ones too no doubt: he recognised Dennis, who'd done opinion pieces for the paper and wrote about the Luddites, and members of the poetry club who met in the Victoria, and then the various creatives who'd been loitering around Martha's garden. And also

Peter, thank god, schmoozing with the various council members who could bring themselves to turn up. He finished the coffee he'd been drinking - there was no alcohol for some reason - and threw the polystyrene cup into a bin then went over and expertly extracted Peter from his cohorts.

"Afternoon Commissioner," he said. "Was your wife stirred all this up, wasn't it?"

"She had a hand in it," Peter replied, "what do you think?"

"Oh excellent. We can really use it to promote the town .. what I really want to do is snag an interview with one of these authors though, look there .. that's Beamish isn't it?"

"Seriously Vollet, are you asking me?"

"Of course, I wouldn't expect you to know you philistine. I think you can tell the authors from the publishers because they're wearing jeans. Yes, that's Beamish, he wrote Credit, and Abi Wells, she wrote a collection of dyke love stories I found quite touching."

"Jesus to fuck."

"And Ronnie Riggs, representing the scatalogical proletariat. He actually sounds like someone from a Beamish story, now that I think about it."

"You're like a teenager at a bloody rock concert. What I need to know, can we use this to get a City of Culture or something, bring in some funding and fill up the teashops for the weekend."

"Feeling the need to justify your post, are you?"

"A few glossy brochures would help me, that's all I'm saying."

"You've got the critic from the Overlooker here and the Regal, that's got to help, if we can feed them a quote .. "

" ... this puts us on the cultural map ..."

"Something more original perhaps, but yes, along those lines ... oh hello, i think we're starting .."

And indeed, some members of the audience were shuffling towards the seats that had been arranged before the stage, overhead lamps illuminating it just as lights in the rest of the hall dimmed. Peter and Vollet made their own way down a central aisle and took chairs in the third row, as the backdrop to the afternoon's proceedings was revealed. Sheena came on and undid a tie so that the embroidered tapestry they'd been working on unfurled and rolled down the back wall, waving around a little before settling. There was a puzzled murmur from the some of the crowd, and it would be fair to say that not all of the tapestries elements held together - so that its militant angry women were prancing among cupcakes and kittens and for some inexplicable reason antiques expert David Dickinson was peering over a wall in the background. Then the music came on, a vibrating drone that gradually increased in volume and Olympia pirouetted onto the stage. She was wearing a black leotard, top hat and bowtie, with a monocle painted around one eye. She came to a stop facing the audience, or would have done except for some slightly misjudged timing, which meant she had to turn a couple of extra steps. Then she held out her palms in front of her, arms half bent and alternately thrust them forward. "Business," she called out as the left hand went forward. "Money," with the right. "Business, money, business, money, business, money."

Martha was waiting just out of sight to the side of the stage, along with Olive and Deborah, two other ladies from the hub. They were all giddy, firstly about the rather awed reaction to the tapestry, and now about the part they were ready to play in the performance. Martha trembled with excitement and nerves. It was her opportunity to show that she was brave and free, that EVERYBODY could be brave and free. To this effect, she wore a leotard also, this one green, and so as to portray a flower, the neck of this was fringed with large floppy petals cut out of white foamboard, and she wore a yellow swimming cap on her head. She was a daisy, while Olive and Deborah were tulips, their faces sticking out of ovals cut into their red foamboard headpieces which rose from the short green petula collars of their own leotards. On the tenth repetition of 'money', Martha capered onto the stage.

"But sir," she trilled, "what about me? I need to bloooomm."

Olympia affected a masculine, sinister laugh. "Ha ha ha ha. I see no profit in you, silly flower. Better for me you be a cabbage or potato, something I can sell."

"But would it not please you to see me dance?"

'Please god, no,' thought Deliah. She and Malcolm had arrived just as the audience were taking to their seats and had placed themselves in the back row. In front of her she could see people holding up their phones and recording. She had flung on an old pink sweatshirt and jeans in place of her school uniform and now tried to shrink anonymously into the back of her chair, but there was no doubt by tomorrow this would be on youvid. And although she knew all her concern was meant to be with Clara and what had happened, for that moment, selfishly, what was going on in front of her right seemed even more mortifying. She glanced over at Malcolm. He had a sort of fixed, grim expression on his face. Impossible to guess what he was thinking except that he was not happy. Martha had been joined on stage by Deborah and Olive and some jaunty flute music had started. They danced around Olympia in a circle, jumping simultaneously at the end of every bar. Certain members of the audience were trying not to laugh and there was a general feeling of embarrassment. Vollet glanced over at Peter. He seemed uncomfortable.

"Stay there," said Malcolm and headed towards the door leading to the toilets. He was aware that under normal circumstances he would have handled this differently, no doubt by persuading Deliah to make a statement to the police, but his mind was frayed around the edges, yet very sharp and immediate in the middle. He felt the determination - the need - to sort this out himself. As he left the room, he heard Olympia crying out, "Oh, the beauty!! "....

The corridor from which there was access to the toilet was deserted, so he ignored the facilities and went to another door further along, labelled staff only. It was unlocked and led into a second corridor, off from which was an office, kitchen, storage room and the door leading to the stage. He found Frank sat on a chair in the office, gazing lazily at the ceiling, smoking one of his rollups. There was a plastic bag taped around the smoke alarm. He looked up surprised as Malcolm opened the door, then smiled delightedly, but not in a nice way - delighted for his own personal amusement.

"Malcolm," he laughed, "what are you doing here?"

"Where's Terence?"

"Terence? Why Malcolm?"

"Because he needs to answer some questions."

"Does he? Why does he need to do anything? Because you say so? I don't think so."

"Because if he doesn't I'm going to go right onto that stage now and announce he's a paedophile, you see if I don't, you, you ... KNOBHEAD!" he spat this last bit out as though it pained him.

Frank raised his eyebrow. "Well, I can see you're worked up. I better go and get him so we can work this out." He stood up and walked past Malcolm, then suddenly turned and shoved him into the room, pulled out a key from his pocket and locked the door, trapping Malcolm inside. It was about time for the reading anyway.

The performance had come to an end. Martha turned round to the audience. They were very quiet. After a painfully silent minute there was some sporadic polite applause. She walked uneasily off the stage, back out of sight to the wings, followed by the others. She turned anxiously to Olympia, her face genuinely stricken, still in the headpiece and swimming cap.

"They didn't like it did they?" she said.

"Oh, I don't know," Olympia replied casually, "Some of them thought it was funny."

"F -funny. They thought we were funny?"

"Of course, they were thought you were fucking funny. It's a joke isn't it .. the 'Hub'."

"Whhatt?"

"It's the same everywhere we go. All these people who want to be 'artists', but only as a cosy risk free option. None of them willing to make the trade off, in terms of security. You think we were performing The Rites of Spring out there? People didn't walk out because they were shocked Martha, we were just wasting their fucking time."

Martha looked rather horrible, as though something nasty had been ripped out of her torso and then shown to her.

"Look at my brother," Olympia continued. Frank was ambling his way onto the stage. "He had one really clever idea, when he was young, a moment of inspiration. Then there were no more ideas, ever, nothing from then on. Now that's cruel. Really cruel. But you and Malcolm, found your real role as muses. This should be good, you need to watch."

The audience, who seemed to be vaguely insulted by events so far, pulled themselves back together as Frank walked on to the stage, bringing a podium with him. For the literati, there was the general feeling that the provincial nonsense was over and done with and now was the chance to witness something they could really get their teeth into. For the local populace there was curiosity and a readiness to be impressed, to see what rare creature might have been nesting among them all this time.

"So that's what an author looks like is it?" asked Peter. He was trying to get over his embarrassment for Martha and was ready to make the evening's central attraction a target for his disdain. And Frank had hardly gone out of his way to make an effort, merely exchanging his jumper for a chequered shirt and attempting to comb his beard. His glasses sat lopsided in his face. He took a folded sheet of paper from out of his shirt pocket and pressed it out flat on the top of the podium.

"A man," he read aloud. "Stuck in his car behind a herd of cows, the verdant lanes seem to him now a hindrance, the unhurried ways of nature for which he mortgaged his existence an irritant in their refusal to submit to the laws of logistics. The neighbourhood has not yet been ordered for him, contrary to expectations, and to his entreaties, his appeal for clemency, the cattle stare back at him through the windscreen like docile unresponsive mothers. What does she think this cow? Of this gesticulating simian entrapped in a cage of metal and glass. The cow goes to make milk for its child, the man .... his purpose is unclear, even to himself, most of all to himself ..."

The critic from the Overlooker sighed and checked his watch.

"At the Gazette he used to wear a trenchcoat and a beret and use a cigarette holder," Vollet whispered.

Disconcerted by the lack of reaction to the prose so far, Frank tried the other side of the paper.

"WHATS THIS?" he abruptly shouted. "MY DVDS ARE IN THE WRONG ORDER, BRAIN FIZZLE, BRAIN FIZZLE.

LOOPY GO I. ART MAKES ME SCREAM/POPPADOMS IN THE ROSARY/MY WIFE IS A PUBLIC RIGHT OF WAY, NO DOn't TREspass!!!"

Malcolm got the door open at the sixth kick, twisting one of the hinges. It slammed open, rebounding off the corridor wall. With each kick he'd become angrier and angrier. He was delighted to become angry, feeling it unspooling out of him with a gathering momentum and now he had absolutely no control over himself marching to the door that led to the stage and he could hear Frank say:

"Mad Malcolm, watch him caper in the fields, happy now to be a cow. How now brow ..."

"AAAAAAAAAAARRGHHHHHHHHHH""! he screamed, hurtling across the stage and throwing himself around Frank's neck in a rather unpracticed tackle that all the same was surprising enough to drive them both to the floor, along with the podium which toppled over with a clatter. He started flailing with some punches - "FUCKFACE!!" he screamed, until Frank shoved him off and rolled away and Malcolm got to his feet and started getting in with some kicks until Frank, still on the floor, grabbed his foot and pushed him away again.

Deliah, who's sense of betrayal had been rising throughout the reading, felt a sudden burst of joy as her father burst out of the wings and knocked Frank off his feet. "YESSS!" she yelled, jumping to her feet and gripping the seat in front of her. Some people in the crowd were still recording the events onstage of course. The critics and publishers appeared to be less than impressed, as though it were all rather ridiculous and beneath them. Only Beamish, Wells and Riggs looked to be entertained, while most of the locals were shocked.

Malcolm was chasing Frank around the stage now, snarling and denying the man a chance to get to his feet and hence reducing him to scurrying.

Vollet glanced at Peter a second time. He looked like a man witnessing a disaster but lacking the necessary training to intervene. He waited until the appalled gasps from the crowd had died down into a disapproving hum before trying to speak to him.

"Well," he ventured. "I guess this puts us on the map alright. Just not in the way we were expecting."

"You understand," Jonathon, Malcolm's director at the firm was saying. "It's not just the video. Although I believe that's what they call a 'youvid sensation'. It's the other story. It was Davenport's cronies who dropped you first, but now there's none of our clients will work with you. The rumour is you're not well. And then there's the allegations of financial mismanagement on the part of your wife, the five thousand she took from the hub and put in your account. Even your parents in law are keeping their distance. We can't possibly keep you on. In fact, it's possible you may not even keep your charter. If I'm being straight, I'm not really sure what you're going to do Malcolm."

Malcolm was only half listening. The first thing was to sell the house of course. There wasn't much mortgage left, but they would be living separately and a lot would be eaten up by Martha's legal fees, if it came to that. Yes, it was a mess and he wished he could take it seriously, but his head just felt empty like a balloon. He looked out of the window of the office and imagined floating.

That would be nice he thought. Just float and float and never feel anything.

5. Paradise lost

"Most men lead lives of quiet desperation, is that not so?" Malcolm Hinchcliffe was saying to a group of clients. They were in the grounds of what was once a manor house belonging to a minor member of the aristocracy but was now a kind of motel/conference centre. He was espousing the core principles of his motivational doctrine: The Hinchcliffe Way. "And they die with the song still inside them - that's what the man said. Well, no, that's not good enough, is it?" There was a murmur of assent from the assembled men, most of them in sales or looking to start up their own business, one or two in genuine emotional crisis. "I have a song inside me, but it's not just a song, it's a ROAR! A roar of strength, a roar of affirmation. And so do you. That's what I want to hear today. Come on ROAR for me!" There was some half hearted, rather reluctant roaring.

Malcolm laughed. "Feeble, yes? But don't worry, that's just what I was expecting - because society has strangled us. It's made us afraid to ROOOARRRRRR!!" and here he threw back his shoulders and did indeed roar loudly and without reserve, so much that some people stepped back in surprise. "It's not a songbird inside you men, it's a bloody lion. That's what they don't want you to know - there's a goddamn beast inside you. Its terrifying and its noble and once you release and tame it it you can do anything, SO come on, fucking rooar for me!!" There was roaring a bit more confident this time. "YOure a fucking lion what are you?"

"I'm a lion. "A lion." "Lion."

"Roarr, FUCKINGG ROARRR!"

Everybody roared!!!!

"YESSS!!" Malcolm shouted. "Now get into your gym gear people we're off to the fucking assault course!!" The assault course was staked out on the lawn behind them. There was netting to crawl under, ropes to climb, hurdles to leap and last of all a small fire to jump over, which was the ever popular photo op. In the evening there was yoga. Malcolm was charging a thousand pounds a head and doing well.

It was the video that had launched his career eventually. He always started off his talks, one night affairs separate from the full length course, by showing it - him tackling Frank and facing off with him. Then he would laugh self-effacingly and feign embarrassment. "But that's when I realised there was something else inside me .." he would say. The audience lapped it up. Many of them had copies of his book - A Year in Hell. It was a modest but regular seller.

"Proud of your old man then, now he's a writer?" asked Malcolm later. Him and Simon were at the bar, in what must have been a ballroom at one time. In fact, Simon remembered having been told that they shot some scenes from a Jane Austen adaptation here. The ladies and gentry doing a quadrille or whatever the hell in their gowns and cumberbands, trying to wed off their daughters like prize heifers. Hard to believe now that life had really been like that once, but he supposed it must have been. "I am as a matter of fact," he said. "Good for you."

"Well, yes, it was ghost written most of it. I came out with my story and some supposed English major transposed it into words. Still, my story though."

"Our story actually."

"I was fair wasn't I? Fair on your mother."

"I thought so."

"How is she?"

"Since having Frank's kid?"

"Yes." Frank looked down abashed at his drink, a Jamesons.

"Better now. The video haunted her for a while, but less people recognised her once she moved away. I suppose wearing that swimming cap helped. It's strange though. It was uploaded as a mockery, but there was a diehard cabal of art feminists came to her defence, applauding her for breaking out of her constrictions. She got a job out of it, raising funding for the Arts Council."

"So, it worked in her favour?"

"Hard to say. There's a lot that still smarts. Losing the house, seeing the For Sale sign go up. That's what was traumatic."

Malcolm looked ashamed again. "You've been to see her?" he asked.

Simon nodded. "Will you?" he replied and sipped his own drink.

Malcolm stared down at the floor and shook his head. "I can't yet," he said. "I cleared her legal fees and that's enough. No reason for me to go and stare at her little ginger bastard is there? And acknowledging the matter would hardly be good for business. The image, you know .."

Simon looked at him. "It's up to you," he said frankly.

"What about Oliver?"

"No, he won't either. Concentrates on the business."

"A fashion empire. Who'd have believed it?" Malcolm looked back up again, his eyes shining with pride.

It was Simon's turn to become distant. "A landfill empire, don't you mean," he said.

"Oh yes, I forgot," said Malcolm, "you're an eco-warrior aren't you?"

"I'm a journalist," replied Simon amused. "Climate change is one of the topics we cover."

"And they're sending you abroad, this website you freelance for?"

Simon nodded. "The Philippines," he said. "Global warming, rising sea levels or choked in waste. They say some of the smaller islands are disappearing. I want to go see for myself."

Malcolm looked at him and his eyes became softer. "I'm proud of you too, you know," he said, "but just be careful out there. I tell my clients they're lions, but I still wouldn't put them in the bloody jungle."

"It's not a jungle dad."

"Well, you know what I mean .. " Malcolm took another sip of his drink, then looked away, a deliberate look around the ballroom. "What about Frank," he asked, "did you hear anything about him?"

"Just that his book deal fell through, and Terence had to sign the sex offenders register. Aside from that, its like the three of them simply disappeared."

"Marth ..", his voice went dry. He gulped and tried again. "Martha .." he got out, "she doesn't see him then?

"Not as far as I know."

"Not even with the .. "

"The ginger bastard?"

"Yes."

Simon shook his head. "She raises him on her own, I think."

Malcolm looked relieved "I might one day," he said. "I might go see her." SImon downed the last of his drink and put the empty glass on the bar. "When I get back," he said, "I'll talk to her. Tell her what you said." He looked at the ballroom himself. Out through the tall narrow mullioned windows he could see the clients negotiating the makeshift assault course, crawling through the netting and climbing up ropes. One of them was stuck.

"It's not a million miles away that they make this shit," Brocka was saying. They were on the beach looking at a drift of plastic slurry, brought in by the tide. He had picked out a small plastic toy - some sort of bug eyed alien with a ray gun. "Indonesia, Malaysia. Just think, some poor bastard in a factory, mind numbing twelve hour shifts pumping out thousands of replicas of Buggo here. Put onto a container ship the size of a horizontal skyscraper and sent to the other side of the world. Then what happens?"

Simon grinned, pushing the glasses up the bridge of his nose. "Sold in some discount store to keep some brat quiet for half an hour, then he gets bored and throws it away. Ends up in landfill."

"And shipped back out. Ends up in the ocean somehow for the fish to choke on. Or here. This is the current world economic system, it's based on churning out pointless shit and it's impossible to stop, or everything collapses, we understand this? Then, you're back in the medieval age."

"Sure, it's not like we can feed ourselves anymore. My country has decided it doesn't need fields."

"So, you're fucked. Unless Mr Maitai keeps churning out Buggo. Probably sees him in his dreams, the night before he commits suicide."

"At least he doesn't work for Mogul."

"Explain Simon."

"Someone I heard about in Malaysia. Content moderator, Mogul outsource it, because no one in America could contemplate even the idea of doing the job. Ten hours a day watching and removing violent pornography and beheading videos. Understandably it affected her mental state. She hung herself and livestreamed it."

"It's the new feudalism. Don't be wicked."

"No, don't be wicked. We're just providers, we're not responsible."

"Then again you work for a tech company. You're sort of hypocritical, aren't you?"

"Hey, we edit our shit."

"What about this shit here." Brocka looked at the flotilla of packaging, plastic bottles, components, containers, toys, bleached of colour, faded so it looked unwholesome and nasty somehow, basically indestructible.

"I have another story," said Simon. "On the Atlantic waste field, the one that's bigger than Texas, they've found a bacteria that's found a way to live on plastic, eat it, infinitesimal amounts. How do you think that's going to evolve? A completely new kind of lifeform that's what I reckon, guts made out of plastic, like a shoggoth. I'm talking way in the future of course. And then what about the plastic we're ingesting through our food, are we going to end up as some sort of host or hybrid?"

Brocka stopped what he was doing to look up. "I worry about you Simon sometimes," he said. "I really do."

When he opened his eyes everything was very bright, but moving softly like a wave, some differentiation in the tones of light. Things swam in and out of focus, but Simon became aware gradually that the movement was the fluttering of a pale curtain in the breeze - calico maybe although his vision was blurred - and the walls around it were white plaster and the very bright immense light was the sunlight coming in through the window. He was in a room, quiet except for the breeze and the flapping of the cloud grey fabric. He tried to move and it was intensely painful, a shardlike stabbing in his leg and head and then a pulsating horrible nausea throughout the rest of his body. His mind was hazy and disjointed too and floated separately from the pain in a way that was familiar from medication he'd taken before. He moved his head as much as he could, trying to make out more of the room. He was on a mattress on a metal bedstead tucked in between white sheets and the air was hot and there was a mosquito net. That was all he could make out before he drifted back into unconsciousness.

The second time he awoke someone was pressing a damp sponge to his lips. A feminine hand that his eyes followed up towards an arm and then the woman who was nursing him. He squinted to see her better. She wore a pale blue dress and had a soft South Sea face with a neutral expression. He tried to move again and the horrible pain came back immediately drenching him in sweat. It must have smelled sour, but the sheets stank anyway of urine and faecal smears. He looked again and it seemed like she was smiling.

"You wake up," she said.

"Where?" he panted. The question cost him all his effort.

"You must eat, a little." She disappeared sideways out of his field of vision and he felt an irrational dread until she returned. She had a warmed container of thin soup into which she dipped a spoon and brought the soup to his lips. He swallowed a drop and the nausea overwhelmed him.

"No! Keep down! Keep down!" she yelled.

He vomited a sliver of bile into his mouth but swallowed it again.

"Yes good. Now rest more. But soon I must change sheets." She disappeared again and he slept.

The next time he swallowed a bit more and she looked at him with concern.

"Now you must move, but will hurt much," she said.

"How badly?"

"Leg smashed bad. Two places. Bang on head. Wound in stomach."

"How?"

"Storm. Tsunami."

He looked at her now she was close. There were marks on her face. Old cuts and bruises, healing. She saw him looking.

"No. That was something else," she said. "I hide from storm, only one. Now you move. Roll onto side." With her pushing he tried. His leg was splinted but to move it was like being scraped out from the inside. He screamed, the pale sweat oozing out of him and then lay there shaking. She tugged the dirty sheets out from under him, each yank causing a terrible jolt of stabbing and sickness. Eventually they managed. He was naked apart from his dressings and the splints tied to his leg and arm. She put a gentle hand on him. "Yes. Very good. Brave man. Now the most important is we clean dressing on stomach. Infection very dangerous. No hospitals here, infection you die."

The next week was a haze of insidious pain and fever and sickness, so that it seemed really that it might be easier to die. But whenever he got to the precipice, he found that there was something inside that gripped onto the edge of life. Worse was the weariness which left him in mournful despair and the rambling fever that burned through him at the end of the week, during which he remembered shouting but could not recall what, or for what reason. Then it went and he was weak, but it was morning and the breeze was still blowing the curtains and there was a bird cawing outside and from the rich scent he could tell there were trees and flowers out there. Later, the woman came in, wearing a pale green dress this time, with a bowl of water for washing and the sponge. By now he was wearing an improvised gown, cut out of a bedsheet.

"Ah, you live!" she said, seeming pleasantly surprised.

He nodded. He was pale, waxy, with long hair now and a matted beard. But alive. "You. Your name?" he asked with an effort.

She pointed to herself. "Me? .. Pila. You?"

"Simon. I think, Simon .."

"You think? What else you know?"

He thought about it. It was disquieting. "Nothing," he said. "I remember nothing."

She looked unhappy. "Bang on head," she said.

"There's no one else here?"

"Since storm, no."

"You mean?"

"They have party on beach. Big wave come, take them, bring you."

"Party? Everyone?"

"Small island, private."

He knitted his brows, confused. He must have been somewhere before this. He knew it wasn't home, that he was foreign. Home was ... no... Just that this wasn't it.

"Don't worry now," Pila said. "Important thing eat. Eat soup." For the first time he remembered he felt really hungry.

Later she brought in an old hospital crutch that she'd found and he tried to stand but it was too painful. He wanted to get over to the window and see what was outside. Instead, he rolled up the gown he was wearing and looked at the leg. It was gashed horribly, the wound stitched together while he was unconscious, and bent strangely, in a way that suggested the deformity might be permanent.

Pila looked at him with a sorrowful, guilty expression. "I push in bone back as best I can," she said, "but I am not doctor."

He looked towards her and a very tender feeling swam over him. He was aware of being in love. He smiled soppily and she smiled back.

"Patient always fall for nurse," she said. "This normal. Be better soon."

The next day he gathered enough strength to use the crutch and the bedstead to stand and hobble over to the window.. Pila had found a pair of spectacles somewhere that was near to his prescription. She looked even better through them although she seemed amused by his appearance and he guessed they didn't suit him. Outside, he saw a veranda and stone balustrade, beyond that tree tops, palms. There was the smell and feel of the sea, not far but not near enough either to hear the waves. Occasionally the heady perfume of some flower and the call of a tropical bird. Pila came in with food and water and to help him wash, which he didn't mind, being able to do the groin now himself, but he still needed help with the toilet which embarrassed him. Like all such things though you adjusted and she took it matter of factly. Soon after he started asking to wash himself, mainly because he was starting to get an erection when she helped him, but she didn't mind this either and said it was a sign he was getting better. It was their first joke, but that time she left him with the bowl and sponge.

With Pila's help he started making steps around the room. Even when lying on the bed the pain came and went in waves and he spent a lot of time on painkillers. Eventually they made it over to the window, him with his arm over her shoulders and using the crutch, and she with her arm around his waist. This time he could see that there was a bougainvillaea entwined around the curved vaselike columns of the balustrade and urns with citrus trees and a garden below: the palms draped with hibiscus from which a flock of hornbills suddenly flew. The scent of the palms and flowers and sea was powerful and intoxicating, as was the dusky smell of the woman under his arms. He got an erection again. This time matter of factly she put a hand under his robe and jerked him off until he ejaculated gasping against the wall of the room. He had to brace his upper body against the sill so as not to fall. Then he got the strength back in his good leg and she put her head on his shoulder and they looked at the view together.

She came back again in the middle of the night. It was hot, balmy, with the calico fastened down against insects that occasionally batted against it but still traces of silver moonlight coming in around the edges and then there was mosquito netting around the bed and the calls of strange animals and birds outside and the hum of the insects. Her hair was down and she wore a sarong which she unfastened as she came over to the bed and she lay down and they kissed and touched each other for a long time, and normal sex was still too painful for him to attempt but they masturbated each other and then lay naked. He stroked her face, the fading marks and thought to ask but instead said: "Isn't anyone coming, to the island?"

She shook her head. "No, I don't think so."

"But they'll be looking for people, the ones who are missing."

She shook her head again, thinking about it. "Not here. This island private, not exist."

"Not exist? What do you mean?"

"Is private, for party. Rich sex tourist."

"Oh."

"You are upset."

He thought about it. "No, I'm not actually. Not upset at all. Is that how you got the marks?"

She nodded. "I not sleep with many men yet. Not do bad things. This is why they hit my face. So, I am inside when God sends the wave. It kill them and send you. God bring you to me and so I try do good."

"Well ... " he started, but didn't know how to continue. It would be too rash at this stage to rationalise. He felt .. not happy, because of the pain, but on the edge of life in some way and full of keen, sharp feelings that seemed to have some deep undertow. "I wish I could tell you about myself," he said.

She looked at him. "Yes. You are from Eng -land."

"Yes, but .." he was aware that all his ideas of England were from films or books and none were from his own memories.

"The woman who brought me here said I might meet a prince from Eng-land, but I do not think you are him."

"No, neither do I. I suppose then they would be looking for me. Where are you from? Family?"

"An island. I won't tell you the name. My father .. not want to know me."

"I want to know you. All of you." They kissed and touched again, all over and everywhere they wanted.

"Yes," she said.

They were out on the veranda that looked out over the garden and the surrounding landscape, lounging on wicker chairs. By this time they had convinced themselves that no one was going to look for them and they had the island to themselves, until somebody, perhaps somebody paid to bring over supplies, remembered to be curious. The veranda was attached to a villa that was high above the coast, high and far enough so that the wave when it came had dashed around it carrying trees and rubble as though it were just a rocky outcrop. Even the garden had survived, although the landscape beyond had been shredded, more accurately it had been picked up and jumbled, areas of it flattened and the rest of it crumpled, with a drenched sorrowful air. The noise had been tremendous, Pila said, a sinister silence that raised the hackles on her neck, an animal premonition, followed by a rolling tumbling sound that rose and then a rushing grinding whining crash as though the world had collapsed. Then later, when she had the nerve to look outside, the waters were swirling outside like demons at a feast, the leaves of palm trees bobbing on their surface like seaweed. It took them hours to recede and settle and the island slowly rose again like the head of a drowned gasping man. There was no power to the villa, the generator further down the island ruined and the food in the freezer had started to spoil, but still there was canned and dry food to last them several months, and also coconuts and palm hearts grew on the island and they were confident they could learn to forage and fish. Of whatever vessels the previous guests had arrived in, only one had turned up back on the island, thrown inland and now laid on its side like a beached shark. There had been another she said, out at sea and upside down but this had gradually sunk and the boathouse itself was shattered, swept away. So they sat out in the baking sun and took in the scents of the flowering gingers.

"Soon I should be able to make it down into the garden," he said. He was anxious now to build up his strength. There was one well on the island that reached down to the water lens, but it might be necessary to build a still down by the coast. Then also they had begun to make love, and although it was intimate and tender, the risk of reopening his wound meant he was unable to go hard enough at the end to bring them both off satisfactorily. But Pila said it didn't matter, and nothing much did seem to matter in the surreal atmosphere of peace and somnolence they'd created together. He'd taken to studying the birds using some binoculars he'd found - babblers, flowerpeckers and coloured ground doves - making notes and sketches like some kind of Victorian botanist and then trying to befriend lemurs he lured onto the veranda with morsels of food, and then at night he looked at the unfamiliar constellations that filled the black sky overhead, circulating around the moon: Phoenix, Crux and Centaurus. At night, the waves of the ocean could be heard faintly and he was keen to get down to the beach.

"Soon, yes," said Pila. He looked at her legs stretched out from the sarong she was wearing. She was weaving some sort of hat from dried bamboo leaves and decorating it with flowers.

"Is that for me?" he asked.

She smiled. "One each," she said.

He smiled back. "I look forward to being useful that's all, making a spear and catching fish."

"You want be Robinson Crusoe."

He smiled himself. "Sure, why not. I have the beard."

"Then you need hat also."

He laughed. "Yes." He looked down again at the garden where two cockatoos had flown over to rest on the branches of a palm tree. "But maybe with feathers not flowers, his and hers."

"Just careful of crocodile."

"You get those?"

"Down in mangrove yes. And macaques in trees. Any animal vicious if hungry enough. Always be careful."

"Even in paradise?"

"Most of all."

He closed his eyes and rested his head against the back of the chair feeling the hot sun beat down. "I don't know if I want to remember or not, what happened before. I might have responsibilities, a family even."

Pila shrugged this off. "Be happy now then, while we can," she said.

He smiled at her and went in for a kiss. "Yes I am happy," he said, "because you are beautiful." The sun beamed down.

He watched her run along the beach, foam splashing around her calves, through the waves where the sea rolled up onto the shore. He limped along slowly behind in his feathered hat, occasionally resting on the crutch so that it left a series of dimples in the sand. The leg still gave him trouble at night, along with the nagging wound in his side that made an awful knitting feeling sometimes, and both caused him to sweat in a cold, greasy way. There were painkillers but they were running out. Then the sun rose and he was able to put all that to one side and appreciate the day. They made their way down to the beach and he stopped to look at the strange animals they encountered - pangolins and tarsiers. He'd made some traps in the shallows which he stopped to check and now he was pulling out a tamban. He beat it insensible against the nearby rock and held it up to show Pila and she gave him the thumbs up, which felt good. Heck, he thought, maybe she could have done that herself and wasn't it ridiculous to feel proud, playing the hunter gatherer. Still, it felt good. Why not play? He put it in the bucket they'd brought with them and looked back up. She was coming back in towards the shore and waving him over.

About halfway up the beach there was a metal post with two links on the side, embedded in a chunk of concrete, uprooted must have been by the storm.

"Net for tennis," she said, and pointed towards where an outcrop of rock and dislodged palms shielded a bay on its far side. "Over there where they make party and Boom! Wave hit."

He nodded and assessed the fallen trees for firewood. He'd found a machete along with other tools in one of the outbuildings, and he remembered, there had been sports equipment down in the basement, along with another door he couldn't get into. It had been made of thick steel and none of the keys on the ring he'd found in the kitchen fitted and there had been a faint blue glow coming out from underneath it. He'd pressed his ear against it and heard a vague humming noise. But the generator was dead, that he'd checked.

"What do you know of these people, who owned the island Pila?" he asked.

"Not much. Friend of Marcos one time. So girls told me. Maybe true, maybe not."

Marcos, he searched his brain for that. "Crazy dictator, wife famous for shoes while people starve, like Marie Antoinette." She gazed carefully at his expression. "He always collect guests and girls himself. Only him and stooges know island location. I think we safe."

"But we should see if we can get that boat working, just in case."

"Maybe, yes."

He sighed. It seemed like the modern world was always restless and never completely left you alone.

"This is what he left behind," said Brocka to Malcolm. He handed Malcolm a large khaki travelling bag. It contained spare clothes, Simon's wallet and passport, a book of course - Victory by Conrad - his notebooks, a tablet, shaving gear etc. They were in a hotel room in Manila. It was hot, dusty. Malcolm had got the news Simon was missing while still in Australia, where he'd been taking part in a tv programme - Survival with Raww Dogg - competing with other contestants as they took part in a series of trials set in the outback. So far it had not gone well, and the most watched internet clip from the series was of him running away from a kangaroo. Which meant that this crisis had come as a convenient diversion in some ways. He'd even brought along his media consultant Mike, who was ensconced in their own hotel over in a separate district - to help publicise the search and find Simon if possible of course - and if it did turn out well there would be at least a second book out of it... But now, from what Brocka was saying, the prospects of it turning out well were minimal and he regretted bringing Mike along at all, feeling slightly sick about it and working out how to ditch him.

"So where was it he went?" Malcolm asked.

"A small island in the north of the archipelago, being washed away by the rising sea levels. He heard about it and decided to make a last minute trip out there before going back home. The tsunami must have got him on the way back."

"You've looked for him?"

"Of course man, went to the island myself. He left three hours before it hit."

"He couldn't have survived?"

"It seems impossible .. hey, I'm really sorry .."

Malcolm groaned and all of a sudden lost strength to his legs and Brocka had to help him over to the bed.

"Ohhh Goddd," he was wailing.

"Hey man," Brocka continued. "I'm sorry, I liked the guy you know .."

"I'll need to go out there."

"Yeah, of course. I'll arrange it."

Simon followed the beach round until he reached a small bay, on the other side of which was a mangrove swamp. He had some traps in the shallows here. He was followed by the lemur he'd recently befriended and that he called Friday. Friday watched and made encouraging chirruping noises as he waded out carefully to check the bamboo cages, testing the ground with his crutch before moving forward and was happy to see that he'd caught some pompano. Among the gnarled roots of the nearby mangrove he could see the plastic detritus that had been washed in by the sea. Much of it had a washed out, unwholesome look like frozen snot. He used the crutch to swirl it around, letting it flounder on the sploshing tide - packets, bottle tops, bags, netting. He felt irked and it reminded him of something. Wasn't it this plastic offal that had brought him here somehow? For some reason the image of a bug eyed alien holding a raygun came into his head. He had no context for it though, it didn't make sense. It was just disturbing.

He had got the boat upright and reckoned it was still operational. He'd even found the keys among those on the ring and all he'd need to do now was cut enough bamboo to roll it down to shore and then of course, figure out how to navigate it. He wondered where the nearest other island was. It was weird. Up until now it had felt like they were the only two people: on their own world surrounded by the sky and sea - like Adam and Eve, it was difficult to avoid the parallel. That they were all alone and could start something new. Wasn't that what everyone wanted - to be the ones who wiped the slate clean? You always gave birth to a Cain though. Who embedded that genetic quirk? His mind was wandering a bit. He culled the pompano, ignored the lapping detritus and waded back to the fringes of the bay. Friday was bounding from rock to rock as though distracted and restless, preparing to abscond.

"Okay," said Simon. "I'm coming." He reached the rocks and looked at Friday, who was chewing on a bit of rind he'd found.

"What do you make of it Friday?" he asked. "All this litter, is it a message from the outside world, the first indication of some parasitic disaster?" Friday simply glanced at him of course and went back to chewing the rind. Simon sighed and taking his catch with them, they followed the coast around, him walking slowly and Friday capering alongside, until they came to the larger bay where Pila was shelling some mussels she'd gathered. They had constructed a makeshift barbeque and so he got the fire going, tremendously hot in the afternoon sun and they cooked the seafood, garnishing it with calamansi lime and drinking coconut milk. At this point Friday finally got bored and disappeared into the trees, so they disrobed and cooled off in the sea, Pila swimming further out while he watched, going only so far as his leg would allow. Invigorated they returned and made love in their stumbling haphazard fashion on a towel on the beach.

"We make baby one day," said Pila, afterwards.

He nodded, laid there looking up at the bright sky. He wondered in that case would they need help.

"Do you think we'll miss other people, eventually?" he asked.

"You get bored of me maybe. We need baby."

"No, never!" he said, looking shocked. "You'll get bored of me more like, looking after an invalid."

She didn't answer that. It wasn't always easy to know what to make of her. So instead, he went through his abstract impressions of the outside world. There were other places out there, Vietnam where they'd had a war in straw hats, against America where they ate hamburgers. That was his idea of the world, a sort of collage of cartoons really. Part of him was curious already, to understand what it was actually like.

"Outside bad, complicated," she said, as though reading his mind.

"You weren't happy there?" he asked.

"Only for very short time," she said, "but mostly no."

He nodded, pained. It could be different though, different if they were together.

"We're in the north of the archipelago," he was saying the next morning. They were out on the veranda. "So we go south, we're bound to meet something aren't we?"

"Oh, so you Sinbad sailor man now, not just Crusoe? Islands hundreds miles apart, yes, you can miss everything, float and die. We stay here!" It was their first argument really. They were silent for a bit. "What you want out there anyway?" she said.

"Nothing except .." he thought of the room with its blue light and then the bug eyed alien. They were connected somehow in his mind. "We can't remain separate from the world. Maybe a hundred years ago that was still a possibility, but not now. Everything needs to be owned with no exceptions. Even paradise has to have a landlord and someone will be coming here someday to settle the account."

"We fight them."

"You think?"

She started to cry. "I don't know," she said. He moved over and held her tightly and their hair tangled and interweaved in the hot breeze that was coming off the surrounding ocean.

"No, me neither," he said.

He rolled the boat down to the beach anyway and gave it a test drive. After some false starts, he figured he could make it go faster and slower, turn left and right, that was about it, but he did a circuit anyway and then tethered it to the metal post they'd found before. Then two days later a storm came down, the torrents of rain pouring against the walls and roof of the mansion. Pila watched it batten down the plants in the garden, causing them to sag like men under a terrible load. Loose petals from the flowers lay scattered and sodden across the paths like damp orange and pink confetti. Neither felt like talking much. She was thinking that he was probably right, but she so wanted not to go. It wouldn't be the same.

That was when Friday capered into the room, shaking his wet fur. He was screeping excitedly. Simon looked up from the armchair where he'd been sitting listening disconsolately to the rain.

"Hey Friday, what is it?" he said. Then Friday did something he'd never been heard to do before. He screeched, a screech of warning. "What?" Simon asked again, then looked at Pila. They were both tense and could see it in each other's faces. He got his crutch and limped his way down the steps to the veranda. He looked out through the pouring rain, there was nothing out there on the main beach. Friday skipped past him and jumped down into the garden. He cursed and used the steps to hobble down and follow him, the downpour drenching him in seconds. From the garden he could see over to the western bay. There was a boat, putting into harbour. He picked up the binoculars from under a table and looked out. Three men, and one had a machine gun slung over his shoulder. They were unloading heavy canvas bags from the boat. He looked back to see Pila on the balcony, the rain sliding down its roof to pour over the edge in spluttering waterfalls. She looked tragic.

"We're going," he said.

The journey out to the island was delayed by the monsoon. Malcolm, Oliver and Brocka were sat in a fisherman's house watching the rains lash the beach. Another local fisherman had taken Simon out to the island before the great wave hit and neither had returned. The island itself they said was completely wiped out, so low now in the water it had been unable to withstand the great wave - people, huts, trees, all ripped up and erased.

"If only he'd gone there after the tsunami," said Brocka. "Then he'd have had a story."

"And there was no sign of the boat, nowhere he could have washed up?" asked Oliver. He had arrived at Manila airport two days ago and despite having business contacts in some of the surrounding countries, found he was able to arrange little that Brocka couldn't arrange better. So here they were, with Martha waiting back home, and although there'd been discussion of her spearheading a media appeal, whatever coverage she received always got linked somehow to that damn youvid clip and undermined the entire seriousness of the situation. So, there was little for her to do but wait, and so far Malcolm had not been able to bring himself to tell her how hopeless the situation really seemed. There'd been bodies washed up, here and on neighbouring islands for several days after the wave, but none of them caucasian.

"We can check the small islands between here and there," said Brocka, "but the news would have spread by now. These people keep in touch, you know. We'll take the plane and circle around anyway."

The seaplane was berthed in a rudimentary hangar at the head of the beach. They took it out once the rains had ceased, flying over the blue ocean, peaceful and limpid now, occasionally crested by a dash of white foam. Brocka had the pilot take it down low over the island. Indeed, it had been obliterated, now just a mound of sand with small abutments of concrete that must have been the foundations of buildings at one time, a few uprooted palms scattered and tossed around like sticks.

"Jesus," said Malcolm.

They were circling the area when Oliver noticed the plume of smoke, very far away, on the horizon.

"What's out there?" he asked.

Brocka looked at the map he'd brought with him. "Nothing," he said. "Nothing should be out there." He said something to the pilot who shrugged. Then he tapped him on the shoulder and said something else. The pilot turned the wheel and they headed towards the smoke. "Let's go look," he said.

The smoke, they saw, was coming from a mansion built near the apex of an unidentified island. One of its walls had been caved in from some sort of blast. There was a garden just below it that was now littered with chunks of charred rubble and beneath that a palm forest still apparently recovering from the great wave. No one knew what to make of it but they took the plane down anyway, landing it on the beach some way below the building. It skidded along for a while, raising up sprays of sand before coming to an ungainly rest that saw them all thrown against the walls of the cabin. Brocka got out first.

"We should check the house," he said.

Malcolm disembarked also and nodded, taking the lead as they walked along the beach until they found a pathway leading upwards. It led them up the slope through a dense but shredded canopy of palms and bamboo until they reached the garden. From here they could see the house with the gap torn into it and smoke funnelling out from the basement where a loose flame occasionally flickered, bothered the air and disappeared. Oliver saw there was a pair of binoculars on a nearby table and looking around saw spent bullet casings spilled across the stone flags. There was a lemur sat on the branch of a palm tree nearby watching them. Feeling nervous they all went up to the house. There were signs that people had been there recently, discarded cigarette ends and water bottles, and then in the kitchen two bamboo hats, one decorated with feathers and the other with flowers. The lemur followed them up the house and watched them for a while, then it lost interest and went away.

They had untethered the boat from the post and run into the sea and clambered onboard as the heavens poured down immense cascades of water upon them. Then they had started the vessel up and chugged away from the beach, accelerating as fast as they were able. They heard gunshots in the distance. Then they were out in the churning waters that tipped the boat from side to side, with the pair of them gripping the wheel trying their best out of instinct to keep the boat level, and then some hours later the monsoon passed and light appeared in the sky and the boat lay drifting on the settled blue waters of the Pacific. They were both exhausted. Simon looked at Pila, wild eyed. Then he stumbled across the cabin and pushed her against its wall and she got out his hard member and spread her legs and he fingered her crotch until it was slippy and let his member push its way inside her bit by bit and they kissed savagely as though they wanted to consume each other and then once it was in fucked rapidly until they both came hard and he felt the wound tear inside him and didn't care and Pila cried out towards the endless sky and waters.

Later on, they were in a bar in Laos and Pila asked the bartender to turn the television to CNN. Simon saw his own photograph, although clean shaven and fresh faced so that no one else in the bar seemed to notice the resemblance. Then photographs of Malcolm and Oliver. The headline: mystery deepens in search for online fashion mogul's missing brother. Then there was a picture of his apparent mother and a video clip of some women dancing dressed as flowers and another of his father running away from a kangaroo.

"So that's who I am," he said.

"Yes," said Pila. "What you feel?"

"It doesn't feel like it makes sense," he said. His side was burning again, probably infected. "I don't know if it was real."

Pila sipped her rum and coke.

"Maybe not," she said.

6. The only way is up

Eustace was in his Whitehall office putting documents through the shredder. There were stacks of files all around him, these having been taken out of their cabinets in the secure storeroom and arranged now in piles on the floor. He was going through them with his assistant Lionel. Most went through the shredder and then the tangled remnants were stuffed into binliners, but occasionally he would carefully select some papers from out of a file, or Lionel would hand some over with a quizzical look and these would be carefully placed into a briefcase the clasp of which contained a combination lock.

They were partway through their task when the phone rang. Lionel picked it up, listened then held the receiver to his breast.

"It's Derek," he said.

Eustace thought about it for a moment, then motioned for Lionel to pass him the phone.

"Derek," he said, into the mouthpiece.

"So, it's true then," he heard the man say, "Blunt accepted your resignation?"

"Yes, so it would seem."

He heard Derek murmur something then say louder, "It's bullshit, you know."

"The man did he what he had to do. I bear him no ill will."

"Its bullshit, all we did to put him where he is. All that policy we hacked out in committee halls, being yelled at by union leaders, jeered at by anarchopunks in dank pubs, my god .. having to listen to Ozric Tentacles. All those deals we figured out in back rooms."

"It's done."

"It's not done, you know that. Those deals we made, it will be many decades before the ink dries on those."

"Our names aren't on them though."

"No, let's hope not. It's Keane isn't it, pushing you out?"

"Blunt needs him at the moment, more than he needs me, that's all it is."

"And it's impossible to keep you both?"

"It's impossible for both of us to keep the promises we made. Turns out, there is only so much money after all .. and the bind he's in with the Americans, he needs the press on board more than anything."

"It's those fucking towers isn't it?"

"It is indeed those fucking towers."

"So Keane gets his department. The man was meant to be a secretary. Now he has more clout than anyone in the actual Cabinet."

"Yes, it's annoying."

"And the money we had earmarked goes towards bribing the press."

"Favourable opportunities will be suggested to their investors, is what you mean."

"Opportunities that we had already handed out."

"Like I said it's annoying .." he paused while Lionel fed more documents through a shredder. Looking round he saw that they had already filled a dozen bin bags.

"Those people are not going to be happy with us."

"No such thing as a risk free investment, Derek."

"It's just I'd rather been counting on their support, in my application for the judiciary."

"Don't fucking whine at me Derek, at least you still have a job .. last time I checked."

"So, what are you going to do?"

"There's consultancy work I suppose, lobbying."

"That could be useful, that might appease some people."

"Yes ... " Eustace thought about it. It didn't feel the same. There wasn't the joy of being next to power.

"So, you'll be in touch?"

"I will." Tired of the conversation, he brought the phone nearer to a shredder and motioned Lionel to feed through the last of the papers he was holding. "Listen ... Derek .. its hectic, we'll speak properly later, yes .. yes." Then he handed Lionel back the phone to put in its cradle. He stepped back and surveyed the cluster of filled bags.

"So, what do we do with this lot?" he asked Lionel.

"I'll burn it in the backyard. Shame it's not bonfire night really. We could have made an effigy of Keane and used it as a Guy Fawkes. Have my kids around waving sparklers."

"That vicious motherfucker, you'd have been better off waiting until Halloween, pass him off as a ghoul."

Lionel picked up one of the bags. "And there was nothing among all this lot, we could use against him?" he asked.

Eustace shook his head. "Nothing significant," he said, "and there's no good delivering a glancing blow, someone like that, it has to be a KO or nothing. I'm telling you this going forward. He'll have tabs on you, so keep your head down. We bide our time, that's all."

"You'll be back," said Lionel.

"Maybe," said Eustace. He looked around the room unhappily. Then went over to the desk and shut the briefcase, hearing the lock click and scrambling the combination before picking it up.

"And those?" asked Lionel.

"I'll find somewhere safe for them. You never know do you, when you're going to need a bargaining chip."

"No, I don't suppose you do."

Eustace left the office and went down into the street, leaving Lionel to carry down the binliners and put them in the trunk of his SUV. He went down to Trafalgar Square, past the great Palladian white stone and red brick buildings of Whitehall, waited with the crowds milling around Nelson's Column with its four stone lions until he managed to hail a black cab, asking the driver to take him down to Worlds End.

So it was, Eustace found himself back in his sister's office. As ever it was crammed with boxes stuffed with files and spare carrier bags. Simone looked at him from the other side of her desk, the bun in her hair drawing her forehead back tight. She was smoking a cigar.

"So you found a place for Andrew after all?" she said.

"On the advisory committee for regeneration in the north of England, his clients are going to be able to glut themselves. One of the last things I was able to do. How fares his marriage?"

"They managed to keep a respectable front for the first year, now the delectable little tart's spreading it about a bit, along with your nephew. The media regards them as rather Z list celebrities. Not that any of that matters to you anymore."

"Keane knew about it. Told me he was going to explode it all if I didn't hand in my notice. An expose of corruption amongst a small coterie of former and existing civil servants, courtesy of his friends in the media. Use it as an excuse to gut various departments and fill them with his own supporters."

"Blunt wouldn't back you up."

"He can't afford to, with his own ministers casting doubt on this weapons business. The party has to look scrupulously honest in all areas, with everyone calling bullshit on the case for war. And they need the press onside - they need to hand them some goodies. That's how I reckon Keane sold it anyway."

"Well, you don't need to worry about money. Your cut from the whole property thing is offshore. I just need to give you the access key, that's all." The clouds of cigar smoke hung in haze between them. She tapped the ash into a coffee mug in front of her.

"That's fine, but what am I going to DO. You picture me on a beach Simone, sipping cocktails all day?"

"No, because there'd be a woman in that picture. A normal woman I mean. Not the one in Stepney."

"There are times, Simone, when I think you know TOO much. What was it, can I ask, between you and your husband. How come you always end up knowing everything?"

"My husband," she laughed. "Well .. he always liked to keep a certain moral distance between himself and his defendants. My attitude was a bit more .. flexible. Then one day he walked in on something that shocked him and the divorce ensued .. that's all I can say really."

"Jesus, that's enough." He waved it away.

"Which brings us to the quid pro quo."

"Yes," he mumbled, "I suppose it does." Still, he hesitated, watching the smoke drift around for a while. Then he unscrambled the combination on the briefcase, took out a pink file and handed it over. Simone opened it up and leafed through the papers inside, occasionally picking one out to examine it more closely. Her eyes quickly became hungry and greedy, for the first time she displayed signs of noticeable avarice. "Oh yes," she said, "oh yes, that's very useful." She closed the file, opened up the top drawer of her desk and placed it inside, next to a deck of tarot cards and a copy of the Financial Times. Then she took some keys from out of her inside jacket pocket and unlocked the smaller drawer underneath, taking out a computer disc and handing it to Eustace.

"You want to look at that here, or in private?" she asked.

"I don't know if I want to look at it ... at all," he said.

She laughed again. "Well, that's up to you. It's strong stuff admittedly, but from what I understand, you're looking to start a war. You're not going to do that with candy floss are you?"

"No," he held the disc between two fingers, "no I suppose not." He hesitated, placed it in the briefcase and locked it again.

"So," asked Simone, "are you planning to see our parents at some point?"

"I'll go over. Father enjoys his new post I gather."

"Oh, he revels in it. Has about three different lord mayors, scurrying to him asking for favours."

"Well, it keeps him occupied, and mother enjoys the kudos it brings."

"Yes, you won her approval at last."

"I did, didn't I?" He nodded contentedly. "I just hope now she doesn't go back to being disappointed again."

"You haven't told her yet?"

"Not yet. It's ridiculous isn't it, I'm nearly forty yet still I dread seeing that look of narrow assessment on her face."

Simone laughed and stubbed out the cigar on a small saucer next to the cup. "Personally," she said, "I built a wall between us. I found it works quite well."

Back at his apartment Eustace paced around for a bit. It felt different. Before, there was always the anticipation of some visit, some 'friend' or petitioner expecting a favour from him or Andrew or maybe even Simone. Not Martha of course, with her quiet life up in the provinces. Now it seemed more lonely, there was time to fill all of a sudden. He studied a chess problem he'd set up, then tried reading - a biography of Thomas Cromwell. A sage advisor, risen from humble origins, eventually to be undone by the unreasonable caprices of the king. He sighed. Found his wallet and flicked through the business cards he'd taken from various Whitehall phone boxes. None quite tickled his fancy and Stepney seemed out for a while. Dammit, he thought and got his coat and went out into the mist and rain, walking until he was over the Albert bridge and into Kensington, down a cul de sac of Georgian townhouses until he'd reached his club: 'the Carrington'.

The porter in the lobby took his moist coat and he passed through some double doors into the privileged atmosphere of the Lounge, its interior, in ambience and decor, perched somewhere between saloon and study, with walls painted fern green and plush leather backed chairs, bookshelves, portraits in oil and lithographs and baccarat tables. The recently introduced smoking ban was discreetly ignored and skeins of smoke drifted and curled around the mid level of the room.

He nodded at some of the attendant members, ordered an Old Fashioned at the bar and sat down, scouring some of the broadsheets which were arrayed on a table nearby and turned so the sports pages faced upwards. He turned them back over and flicked through. His resignation averaged page six or seven, and no one seemed to have connected the dots to the weapons debacle which was monopolising the headlines. Or they'd been subtly discouraged, it was hard to know which.

Greaves had spotted him and brought over his own scotch and sat down.

"Resigned Eustace, really?" he asked.

"Looks like it," said Eustace, sipping his drink.

"Any particular reason?"

"There's some personal projects I need to work on, apparently."

"So, it's like that is it?"

"That's what it's like."

"Noyes phoned me, he was worried."

"Noyes," he tssked with irritation, "about his rail extension I suppose, over in Barking."

"You did persuade him to put forward the congestion bill, in the belief that the rail contracts would be handed out to some business friends of his. Now he's worried all that will fall through."

"It probably will. The best he can do is tell his friends to keep a tight hold on any paperwork and lobby against the extension until it looks like it's going their way again."

"His constituents will love that won't they, discouraged from driving to work and now they're stuck with their dilapidated tube line too."

"No one asked them to live in fucking Barking, did they?"

Greaves laughed.

"What else, Desmond?" asked Eustace.

"Wanted to talk to your brother. There's these goddamn council flats at the edge of the borough we were forced to build. Now they need renovating. I was wondering .. he knew some way to do it cut rate .. I mean, the rents there are capped and they still expect the place to be liveable .. both parties, tenants and council, resent each other, god knows why they actually put them there in the first place."

"Social inclusion Desmond, everyone has to have a little taste."

"My point is, they'll complain anyway, so if we cut a few corners and save ourselves some pounds, it won't matter."

"Because the borough of Kensington is so deprived. You're worried what, there'll be less money for floral displays and bunting?"

"I knew it was a mistake to let affiliates of the labour party in here. I should have asked them to cancel your membership as soon as you went over."

Eustace laughed this time. "It's a good job for you that I did," he said, "or there might be more flats. All the same I'll talk to my brother, see if this organisation of his knows someone."

"Mucho appreciated." Greaves rattled the remaining ice in his glass and took a good swig. "So what are you going to do? I can get you tickets for the Test match, things get so terribly boring."

"Really, you're espousing cricket as a cure for boredom? I'm a rugger man, you know that."

"Ah .. league I suppose?"

"True to my roots 'n ting, Desmond."

Greaves looked at Eustace with slightly widened eyes and then shook his head sadly. "Yes, those early years," he said, "must have been very damaging. Living in the shadow of the factory spires and forced to eat mushy peas. Still, if you'd condescend to watch a union game, I could get you a seat for the cup final."

Eustace thought about it. Well, there was all that time to kill. "I don't mind hobnobbing," he said, "as long as it's in the executive box of course."

"Mingle with the hooray henries?"

"Sure, why not. Social mobility, Desmond, as we were discussing. Everyone needs a taste." With a rye smile, he raised his glass in quiet salute then took a swig.

A week later he was in a pub with Derek. He was a bit drunk. He'd been drinking a bit too much lately. It wasn't busy, an 'old man's' pub. There was one at the other end of the tap room, reading a paperback with a wet labrador nestled at his feet. He found that he missed the cigarette smoke. Pubs weren't quite the same without that permissive, enabling haze. Goddamn Bland. There had been that wonderful, nostalgic time when everywhere smelt like nicotine, what happened to that? He'd gone to London and there'd been yuppies having liquid lunches, the privatisation documents skimming across his desk, some builders or contract workers getting drunk in the corner ..

" .. it's not going well," Derek was saying.

Eustace snorted.

"They found the analyst who worked on the reports," Derek continued. "He says his work was misrepresented .. skewed .."

"Skewed .. by who exactly?"

"Guess."

"Keane," Eustace spluttered contemptuously. "It's alright being handy with a soundbite, when you're dealing with nebulous material," he said. "People like to have things encapsulated for them, I suppose a newspaper man learns that. My brother, I remember, learnt a whole raft of words you could use to elicit a trained response among the party faithful. Dog whistle politics."

"Even his rivals would say: the phrases he'd give them were so good, they'd have to use them, even when it ran against their direct interests."

"So why won't they tow the line now?"

"He's dealing with cold analysis isn't he. You rearrange it, but it tends to snap back into its original position. Unless you flat out produce a forgery. And his rivals, just because they admire him, doesn't mean they won't take him down a notch or ten. Not exactly blushing violets, newspapermen."

"And the investor's aren't bothered, now the contracts are signed and sealed."

"Why should they be? They're already looking for their next meal."

"It's a bit of a spot."

"Could be."

Eustace thought about it a while, trying to coordinate himself enough to take a drink from his pint of Fuller's. Eventually he reached for the coat which he'd placed on the velour cushioned bar stool next to him and removed a sheet of paper from one of the pockets. There was a blurry image on it, but distinct enough to be unsettling. Derek took it and squinted at it, then the blood rushed out of his face down to his feet, leaving him pale and shuddering.

"That's not .." he stuttered .."that's not is it .. ?"

"It is," muttered Eustace.

"Dear god, that's not ... no ... " He thrust the image face down on the table.

"It's not right," whimpered Derek.

"A man can't have that many orifices, it's true," replied Eustace.

"And what do you expect me to do about .. that. It's way beyond my remit, you must realise .. anyone's remit."

"I was thinking of your position with the CPS, you must have contact with Special Branch."

"You want me to report it to them?"

"No. I want to talk to them, as high up as you can manage."

"I see." Derek polished off the last of his beer. "Goddamn it I need a whisky," he said. He went to the bar and came back with two doubles. Eustace waited and surveyed his surroundings. The white tiles on the lower portion of the walls seemed slightly greasy and yellowed. There was a ceremonial brass plate nailed to the painted wood panels above them next to him. He remembered to pick up the sheet of paper and put it back in his pocket, then Derek returned and they each took a stern drink of their shots.

"Dammit, that's better," said Derek. "You know I was going to suggest we go to Soho after this but I've lost all motivation."

"You could come with me to Stepney."

"No .. it was interesting, but that was a one off for me .. I'm very much a meat and potatoes kind of chap, when it comes down to it. Probably after tonight I'll end up being a bloody monk."

"I need to talk to those people."

"Hmm .. it's an ask .."

"Tell them."

Derek acquiesced. "Yes yes, okay," he said in a rather reedy voice, "But it's your round .."

Eustace woke up the next day in his flat with a dreadful hangover. He was laid the wrong way round on his bed wearing only his shirt and there was some kind of dried salve stuck to his thighs. He buried his head in the sheets in an attempt to muffle his headache. There were slices of pepperoni pizza stuck also to the pillows with encrusted cheese.. Eventually the need for water drove him to the bathroom, where he drank from the tap then forced himself to shower, ignoring the nausea he felt. He washed away the salve, examined the exposed welts and then pulled on some pyjamas and went to sleep again on the sofa. When he woke again the headache had narrowed down to a sharp pinpoint of nagging pain.

He took some paracetamol and washed it down with a bottle of lager from the mini-bar in the main room - hair of the dog, he reckoned. That left him feeling a bit better but now it was getting late and he couldn't sleep. He put some Mahler on the stereo, even tried reading a bit of Wittgenstein, and when that got too much he turned on the tv and watched american cable and then the shopping channel. By mid morning he was making a fried breakfast - bacon, mushrooms and eggs - and then the phone rang.

"We're in the park," said Derek.

He dressed, took the disc from where he'd taped it to the back of the boiler and exited the apartment block, crossing the road to go over to the park. It was still grey and misty and the trees were struggling to hold on to their brown and yellow leaves, most of which were sprinkled across the grass and tarmac pathways, laid there damp or crinkled. He wandered around until he found Derek and a man with clear rimmed spectacles and a dour expression sitting next to him on a bench. The abandoned power station was behind them with its four white chimneys reaching up to the grey cloud covered sky. Derek got up to allow Eustace to take his place and then strolled away, a discreet distance.

"You wanted something?" the man asked.

"You're Special Branch?" Eustace responded. The man nodded.

"Terrorist plots, how many are you aware of, right now."

The man turned his head and stared at Eustace in mild disbelief.

"Because .. we make that information available to anyone who asks," he said eventually.

"You don't I know, but let's say it's more than one. Would that be fair?"

"It's a few more than one."

"Derek told you I had a disk .. I came into possession of a disk I should say."

"He mentioned it yes," the man said quietly, turning round to stare again at the damp leaf strewn in front of them.

"I can ensure all copies are deleted."

"Let me see it." Eustace gave him the disc. "All copies .." the man deliberated, "never know for certain though, would he?"

"I promise to do my utmost."

The man sighed, a little tired. "What is it you want?" he asked.

"These plots, I want you to let one of them through."

The man looked at him again. He had the disc in his hand and was stroking it with his thumb. "Really?" he said, scrutinising Eustace hard.

Eustace nodded, a little subdued.

"Dammit," the man said. "We do that, you know there's going to be all sorts of enquiries."

"But it could end up working for you in the long run, in terms of increased resources, relaxation of the surveillance laws."

"You're in no position to guarantee that."

"Not yet, no."

The man looked at him again. He nodded. "Yes I see," he said. "This goes off, you're counting on an outrage and resistance to the war falling away. But that's no good to you unless the PM knows you're responsible. Now you've given us the idea, why don't we put it forward anyway?"

Eustace chuckled mirthlessly. "Really, you're going to ask Bland to take it on his own conscience? No, no, my friend, this is very much a troublesome priest situation."

The man looked at the disc once more before sighing again and putting it in his own pocket. "And if I decline, or decide to put you and your sister on a red list?"

Eustace tapped the seat before saying: "A copy gets automatically mailed to my acquaintance Dewpepper, from there on in it's out in the wind."

"You're giving us no choice, is that what you think?"

"Of course you have a bloody choice. What I'm doing is letting you all off the hook. These towers, the culprits are all squirrelled away in caves and to get at them is going to take decades, maybe. Long arduous secret service work and nobody can know anything about what you're doing, am I correct? In the meantime, the Americans are supposed to stand around looking like ineffectual pussies? Hardly in their character is it. So, you can't get your hands on the right bastard, you hit the nearest available bastard hard, so people know not to mess. That's just realpolitik, the same rules as streetfighting."

"So, the collateral damage if I let this plot through, you're taking it on your conscience. Our sins on your shoulders, how very christlike," the man said sardonically. All this time Derek was strolling up and down the path, pretending to be texting into his phone.

"What do you think power is exactly, except the taking of the sins of others onto your shoulders. Did you ever read the Grand Inquisitor?"

The man shook his head.

"For dominion over man, first you make them rely on you for sustenance, then you give them a shared mythology, then you offer to take the role of their conscience. It's something our enemies know very well."

The man continued to stare at the path.

"It doesn't matter." Eustace scratched his thigh. "All that matters is you have my proposal. I'll wait a moderate length of time for a response. What would you say a reasonable timeframe was?"

"They can move quite fast. I wouldn't say more than a couple of weeks."

"Two weeks, okay. In the meantime, I'll leave the ball in your court, if that's alright." He stood up and left the man sat leaned back slightly against the bench, eyes narrowed as silently, like a chess player, he ruminated on the situations various likelihoods and outcomes. Ignoring Derek, Eustace walked away from the both of them, back between the trees towards his apartment, gradually becoming an unclear figure in the light mist.

"Eustace, so glad you could make it!" said Bland. It was bonfire night at the PM's gifted, temporary country residence Chequers, dark so that you could see the Elizabethan building just as a dark mass with yellow lamplight peeking out through the curtains of the ground floor windows. The tables in the courtyard gardens were illuminated by candles placed in hollowed out pumpkins, the light flickering out through their carven grimaces, an anachronistic hangover from halloween, but one that cast a soft waxy gleam over the surrounding vol au vents, winter parkin and champagne interred ice buckets, reflecting off the condensed water droplets sliding down their exterior. Pairs of lit flaming braziers led across the lawn to where a large bonfire had been constructed, the taller planks and staves leaning teepee-like against the central stake and stuffed in between with smaller hunks of timber and kindling. Somewhere beyond were the Chiltern hills. People were dressed in deference to the chill November weather, in woollen coats and hats, or at the very least jumpers or cardigans.

"Glad to be invited," said Eustace. They shook hands warmly, Bland with his effortless, sincere smile and Argyle sweater. The pair of them were lit by a string of electric lights that were stretched between the beams of the bowery behind them. There was music coming out from speakers somewhere near the house, some trendy band that Eustace remembered from the early campaigning days. Waterhole, weren't they called? Fuzz guitars and nursery rhyme lyrics in a northern whine.

"But such terrible circumstances." Bland frowned. The bomb had shredded thirty six people in a tube station, twenty three of them wounded and mutilated, the rest dead.

"Appalling," said Eustace. "There'll be a war now, of course."

"Now people see the threat we're up against. It's tremendously regrettable of course, that it takes a tragedy ... but the papers are on board now, and the backbenchers .. hard not to support us now without appearing tacitly complicit."

"That's something I suppose."

"Yes, but like I say, such terrible ..." Bland stood looking at the ground sadly, holding his champagne flute, the music changing now, the old campaign anthem - 'The Only Way is Up' - an uplifting electronic, club dance tune. He laughed suddenly, as the people near to them groaned.

"Remember this, how sick we got of hearing it," he said.

"Yes," said Eustace. "Keane's choice wasn't it, a bloody good one."

"Don't be sore about Keane, Eustace."

"I'm not, after all, we both know ...."

"Know what, Eusto?"

"We go in there, and it turns out there aren't any weapons, someone has to take the blame for massaging those reports don't they?" He noticed that the surrounding conversational hubbub had altered in pitch to signify distracted anticipation and that the people around them had started to follow each other down to the lawn, taking their drinks with them, following the flaming braziers to where the kindling of the bonfire had been lit and was starting to catch. The song continued, reaching its apex:

the only way is up, babeeee, for you and me now ..

"That's harsh Eusto, there's no need for that," Bland scolded. Eustace just shrugged. "Shall we?" he said, indicating that they might want to accompany the rest of the crowd with a nod of his head. "Absolutely," said Bland, taking care to refill both their glasses from a champagne bottle resting on one of the tables, before they descended a set of stone steps, down onto the grass.

"I appreciated your present by the way," Bland said, as they walked between the flickering light of the braziers until they could hear the crackle of the larger fire as it started to consume and feast on the timber. Upon the central pole had been lodged an effigy - not the traditional traitor Guy Fawkes, but instead that old familiar bugbear - Helen Fletcher, who had governed the country during the 1980s, dismantling the unions and imposing upon it free market economics. "First edition of The Secret Agent," he continued. "Bloody interesting read."

"I thought it would be, yes," replied Eustace. Some of the younger, tipsier attendees - a group of aides and interns - had inevitably started to chant "Burn the Witch! Burn the Witch!" Eustace looked around, first, back at the glowering mansion above them, the leering pumpkin faces minute but still visible as the candles burnt down inside them, then at the medieval style braziers and then the effigy beginning to burn and dissolve on the stake - and had the distinct impression of being in one of those old Hammer horror movies. The feeling that something pagan and unknowable had been glimpsed below all their avowed intentions.

"Yes," Bland was saying, as the blaze cast its shifting glare upon their faces and left glints of orange light swirling in their champagne flutes. "I'm not sure we can have you back as an advisor, without it looking odd, but there is a post going in Europe, on the Trade Commission. It would be very useful to have a good man there, very useful, and who knows, that sort of post often leads to a lordship. We need good men in the House of Lords too, very useful."

"A lordship, eh?"

"Yes." Eustace at last took a sip of his champagne and looked around. There were diplomats present, financiers, a theatre director, a pair of academics even. Bland's wife Sheryl was drifting from one group to another, sharing a joke, laughing, or showing an intense interest. Her parents had been television actors, he knew, on a working class soap. Bland's own father an illegitimate lawyer who educated himself out of the shipyards. His trade minister an ex-boxer from the merchant navy. They all had good proletarian credentials if you cared to look. That time, mid century, when there'd been genuine toil and hardship but a way out too, maybe for the first time. An opening. Permission to be free. Was it still there? He looked back at Bland.

"You know me," he said. "I enjoy being useful." Now he saw that Derek was there at the edge of the throng, talking to someone from the Italian consulate, but occasionally shooting a glance in his direction. He excused himself and went over, allowing the pair of them to conclude their conversation before steering Derek away from the gathering to a space where the firelight was more dim, insubstantial.

"You haven't answered my calls," said Eustace.

"Well, I've been busy .." said Derek half heartedly. He looked awkward, skittish.

"Not that busy," said Eustace, staring at him. Up above the music had started again, something sombre this time, Brahms.

"The news upset me," said Derek, avoiding his glare. "This whole business has unsettled me, to tell you the truth .. and then there's our pal Noyes."

"What about him?"

"Found out he's not up for re-election didn't he, and his friends are pressing him, threatening to sue. He's very down about it all."

"I'll square it with his friends, don't worry, and get the rail extension moving too .. once I get the post in Brussels."

Derek peered up at him. "Brussels?!" he said. "That's what you were talking about with Blunt?"

Eustace nodded.

"I see ... I seee. Well, I am sorry for avoiding you. Perhaps I've been oversensitive. Its nerves you know. Always I was a bit of a martyr to them."

Eustace waved it away. "You have to understand. All that other business, the stuff on the disc, it's something outside oneself. You do it, put it away in a box, forget it, put on a suit and carry on."

"Is that how your sister, see's it?" asked Derek slyly.

Eustace only skipped a beat for a fraction of a second. "My sister? No, why."

"Our friend in special branch asked me to pass on their apologies, but it was felt necessary to turn over her shop. More as a formality than anything else."

"Ah well .." Eustace wondered what else Simone had up there among all her papers .. the mind boggled really. "No, the way she sees it, the box is what matters and all this other stuff, the politics is the psychosis. Then again she considers herself an occultist. And of course, it's nonsense."

"Absolutely, it's nonsense. Anyway, come this way, let me introduce you to someone." He led Eustace back towards the inferno, where the whole edifice was now burning voraciously and thick plumes of woodsmoke were billowing across the grounds, carrying their heavy saplike scent with them. The 'guy', a caricature to begin with, was crumbling and collapsing in on itself among the charred timbers, and the top half of its head fell inwards so that all that was left was a sinister twisted grin. The fireworks started, shooting up into the night sky and exploding loudly into a myriad of glittering coloured sparks, making bright patterns like unfolding flowers. The aides were looking up making their 'oohs' and 'ahhhs'. Derek tapped one on the arm and she turned round as a detonating rocket left bright flashes across her face.

"This is Laura," he said, "who's been working in Housing, putting together all those dreary statistics. Going to be part of that regeneration committee your brother's on. Laura, this is the formal special advisor to policy."

Eustace and Laura shook hands.

"So you and Andrew, be working together closely will you?" he asked.

"Looks that way!" She beamed. She was a bright young thing.

"She's very keen," said Derek. "Always working the candle at both ends, I think that's how the saying goes."

"I understand," said Eustace, "bit of an eager beaver, eh?"

"That's me!" she replied, beaming again. The sky above was a noisy barrage of incandescent explosions.

Derek and Eustace looked at each other. "Yes," said Eustace, "I'm sure you'll get on fine ... "

Simone returned to her office to find that the main door had been opened. She looked at it carefully. It hadn't been jimmied, they must have used lockpicks. Same with the connecting door to the staircase. She went upstairs. They hadn't made too much of a mess. Some of the boxes had been turned upside down and the papers flung across the floor, the locked drawers forced open, that was all. Quite considerate really. She started to do an inventory of what was missing, but then thought 'fuck it', they probably just photographed the rest anyway. Maybe it was simply time to move on, somewhere abroad, possibly. She sat down and opened the top drawer of the desk. The pink file was gone, but that was okay. She'd half been expecting the visit, taken out what she needed and replaced it with fluff. Was that what they called it? Now there was just the copy of the Financial Times and the deck of tarot cards. She picked the cards up and shuffled them, then placed them on top of the desk. Then she lit up a cigar and smoked for a while. Then she stubbed it out on the plate which was smeared dirty with ash and cut the deck and started doing a spread. The Hanging Man and nine of swords. She winced. Then to the left she put King of Cups. She tried two more cards. Eight of coins and the Devil.

She picked up the smouldering cigar stub, drew on it until the embers rekindled, exhaled the smoke and leant back to stare a while at the cracks in the ceiling and its paper globe lampshade, the smoke starting to drift around it like coruscant vapours around a planet.

She'd been right. It was time to leave.

Also by Wendell Harris;

The Idle King and Other Stories

Webcomics;

The Ruins of Epsilon Five

Do fembots dream of electric prunes

Printed in Great Britain
by Amazon